CLAS

Also available in the Models series

MODELS
CLASH ON THE CATWALK

CHLOË RAYBAN

Hodder
Children's
Books

a division of Hodder Headline plc

First published in Great Britain in 1997
by Hodder Children's Books

A Catalogue record for this book is available
from the British Library

ISBN 0 340 68163 2

Typeset by Avon Dataset Ltd, Bidford-on-Avon, Warks

Printed and bound in Great Britain by
Cox & Wyman, Reading, Berks

Hodder and Stoughton
A division of Hodder Headline PLC
338 Euston Road
London NW1 3BH

One

The taxi swung round and headed into the Eurostar terminal. Paris . . . Paris! . . . I was actually on my way!

The usual crowd of onlookers did a double-take as I climbed out of the back. OK, I'll come clean with you, I'm kind of good-looking. When nature handed out the goodies, for some reason, I got a whole lot more than my fair share. Like natural ash-blonde hair, cute blue eyes, baby-soft skin and a look like butter wouldn't melt in my mouth. Being noticed doesn't surprise me any more. In fact, it kind of surprises me if people *don't* notice me, if you know what I mean. I'm not big-headed about it or anything. It's just a fact about me.

Anyway, that fact was the reason why I was on my way to Paris. I'd been chosen to be the star of a commercial for a new Klaus Klavin perfume – Ange Bleu. This was my big break. I'd fought for the job – fought hard. 'Cos, I'm telling you, you may think I look pretty good compared to your normal run of rail-travellers, but put me up against a load of professional models and I'm just average – maybe even a bit below average, if I'm honest with myself.

1

But, curiously enough, it was me who was chosen to represent the Blue Angel.

The commercial was being shot by this Italian guy – Julio Iononi – you may have heard of him. He's the one who did all those weirdo ads for knitwear featuring supermodels with their heads switched to animal heads – like Kate Moss was a kind of baby deer and Naomi Campbell was a zebra – it was plastered all over the media last year.

The decision that Iononi had picked *me*, of all people, for the launch ad didn't come till the very last minute. So my exit from London had turned into one big panic. I'd barely had time to pack. I had to pick my ticket up from the 'Today's Departures' Desk and there was a massive line of people there already. Me and my three bags joined the end of it. The people at the head of the queue seemed to be taking forever and everyone behind them was getting impatient and shuffling their luggage forward. And then just as I was getting within striking distance of the desk, this girl blatantly pushed in front two people ahead of me.

'Hey!' I said. But she took no notice.

She just stormed at the Eurostar woman that she'd missed two trains already and wasn't intending to miss this one.

'Would you please join the end of the queue and wait your turn,' the Eurostar woman said, trying to keep her cool.

But the girl wouldn't budge. Then this argument broke out between the guy in front of me – who obviously fancied this girl like mad and wanted to let her in (she *was* kind of gorgeous, actually) – and the one in front of him, who didn't. In the confusion, the Eurostar woman must have given in, because the girl swept past me knocking my bag over as she did so. She didn't pause to say sorry or anything, she just strode on. She was tall – stunning, in a cold, Nordic kind of way. And didn't she know it! Who did she think she was?

We all got on the train in the end, anyway, so I don't know what the fuss was about. I settled down in my window seat and within a few minutes the doors slid closed and the train started to pull out of the station. I was on my way.

As the train rumbled past all those tatty old backyards of outer London I still couldn't believe my luck. Looking back, I started to run through the long hard slog it had been to get to this precise point in my 'brilliant career'. I'll fill you in on it if you like . . .

It all begins way back – a year or so ago in New York. That's where I lived with my Mom – or Cherie, as she prefers to be called. I mean Cherie's OK, really – it's just that she was one of the Seventies icons and, although she's like forty-something now, she can't forget it. Remember that shot of a girl made to look like The Statue of Liberty on the Pirelli calendar? You probably don't 'cos, like most people, you're too young – but that was Cherie. Anyway, Cherie's done loads and loads of *Harper's Bazaar* front covers – she even made it to Hollywood for a while. For her age, I figure she still looks fantastic. She should do, too. You should see the arsenal she keeps in the bathroom cabinet. Sometimes I think it's she alone who keeps 'Charles of the Ritz' in the Ritz. And she's like *really* into working-out, she's even made her own work-out video – which wasn't exactly a sell-out, by the way. She still exercises for a full hour every day. So I've kind of grown up with this beauty ethic thing. Take diet for instance (and *that's* one big yawn). Everything she buys us is Fat Reduced or Low Cal or Extra Lite. I don't think, since I was born, I've *ever* been given anything to eat with its full quota of nourishment – I swear we even drink low calorie water. There was one whole summer when we didn't have anything in the fridge but butter milk and water melon.

Cherie was just so determined that I would grow up to be everything she'd ever fought to be – a kind of two-legged clothes-horse with a fixed grin. Know what? I was already doing babywear shots before I could walk. When I was a little kid, she put me in for all the talent contests going – and I did model competitions all through school – I missed loads. And then, come the time I was a teenager, I turned out to be the number one big disappointment. She sent me to all the people she knew, big name photographers and all. I went to casting after casting but all I got was crummy catalogue stuff. I guess I was skinny enough and had all my features in the right place but I have this really pale skin. Up against all those big, bronzed American goddesses I just looked washed-out. So I used to plaster myself with loads and loads of make-up. You could brave it out in all that yucky catalogue stuff. I'd put on a big brash smile and I guess I made their dumb clothes look pretty much wearable. But frankly, I found standing in front of the camera being second-rate was a kinda humiliating. Guess my heart wasn't in it, and didn't it show!

And then Carl moved in. Who's Carl? He's Cherie's latest conquest and one *big* pain. He just lounges round the apartment drinking beer and watching baseball and stuff. He's useless. He's sponging off Cherie and the worst thing about it is he knows I've sussed him. It's like all-out war between us. I can't do anything about it 'cos Cherie just interprets any negative vibes from me as pure undiluted jealousy. Me jealous of a loser like Carl? You must be kidding! Anyway, ever since he's been around, it's like the apartment's not my home any more. He's always spread out in front of the TV or showering his great useless body in the bathroom or lousing up the kitchen with his crummy takeaways and junk. And he keeps giving me money in a really obvious kind of way to go to the movies, and you can see it's to get me out of their way. So, with the last bit of catalogue money I earned – know what I did? I just walked into a travel agent and bought myself a one-way ticket to London. Time had come to look up Dad.

Dad. OK, I haven't mentioned Dad up to now. Dad was Cherie's number two husband. She met him in the Eighties, Mom's wacky phase, when she was doing a Vivienne Westwood shoot. That's how I came to be born in London, which is kinda handy for travelling around. Once I arrived, Mom and Dad's happy union lasted all of eighteen months. Dad's done the decent thing, of course. He's paid for my education, and dance classes and gym sessions, and clothes and shoes, and top-notch dental treatment and stuff – you name it. And, when he's been on business trips to the States, he's even taken me out for a slap-up meal or two. He sends me real gold jewellery every birthday and Christmas. I've got a great treasure chest of it in the bank. So you can tell, deep down, he really cares about me. So, once I'd got that ticket, I knew I was heading for the parent I could count on.

The flight landed at Heathrow real early, like five in the morning. So I climbed in a cab and told the guy to head over to Dad's address. I was about to give him the surprise of his life.

All the way over on the flight I'd kept picturing myself turning up at his apartment and him opening the door in his dressing-gown and being knocked out by me being there, arriving out of nowhere, and then us having this really cool breakfast together – real bonding stuff.

So the cab turns up at this real swish address. It was one of those great towering old-world terraces with pillars up the front, built like a wedding cake and painted gloss-cream, and there's his name right above his doorbell. I pressed the bell. I waited ages. I figured he must have still been asleep or in the shower or something. I pressed again. Still no-one answered the door. The driver climbed out of his cab: 'What seems to be the trouble, Luv?'

'My Dad doesn't seem to be at home.' I was getting really nervous. I mean, I was counting on Dad being there to pay for the cab and everything. The air ticket had totally cleaned me out. Cab drivers in New York could get really nasty if you didn't have money to pay them. But this one just said quite kindly: 'Your Dad *is* expecting you, isn't he?'

I shook my head. I never cry. But tears started welling in my eyes in spite of myself.

'Come on now, Luv. It's not as bad as all that.'

'It is. You see, you'll have to leave me here. I don't have any money.'

'Know anyone else in London?'

I shook my head.

'Tell you what, I'm parched – just going to break off for a cup of tea, I was. Why don't you join me? Ten to one we'll find your Dad'll be back later.'

So that's how I ended up in this kind of hut in the street with all these cab drivers having a big buttery piece of toast and marmalade and a mug of tea. And they were all really nice and jokey, like I was the biggest bit of entertainment they'd had since Christmas – and they insisted on having a whip-round to give me money when they heard I didn't have any. I would never have believed cab drivers could actually be human like that. They were just so *kind*. Maybe all that stuff they give us in the movies about good old England is true after all.

Dad *wasn't* back when we returned to the apartment. All I could think of was to go to his office. The address was in a place the cab driver called 'The City'. 'The

City' at that time of day was swarming with men heading to their offices looking as if they'd specially dressed up to play the part of the typical English Gentleman – they even had rolled umbrellas, for goodness sake!

Sid (by this time my cabbie and I were on first name terms) said he'd wait outside while I went into the office, and I left him reading a paper with his engine purring.

'Is Howard Garnett in?' I asked the woman on Reception.

'Do you have an appointment with Mr Garnett?' she said, eyeing my ripped jeans and sneakers as if I were a vagrant or something.

'I'm Ashe, Ashley Garnett, his daughter,' I said.

She looked at me as if she didn't believe me.

'I'm afraid Mr Garnett's not available. He's in a meeting.'

'But I've come all the way from New York . . .' I said.

I guess I was raising my voice. She looked embarrassed and got up, saying she would see what she could do.

The next thing was that my father came hurtling down the corridor.

'Ashley . . . Ashe. What on earth are you doing here?'

'Dad . . . Aren't you glad to see me?'

'Of course I'm glad to see you,' he continued, impatiently. 'But I'm right in the middle of an extremely important meeting. You can't just turn up out of the blue like this . . .'

Then he caught sight of my face.

'Have you just flown in? You look terrible.' He put an arm round my shoulders. 'Come on, Baby. Of course I'm glad to see you. But you could have called first, couldn't you? Tell you what: you go back to the apartment, have a shower, get some sleep and we'll talk about this later, OK? Does your mother know you're here?'

I shook my head. 'OK, I'll give her a call. Get Angela to give you the keys and get you a taxi.'

'I've got a cab – I just need money that's all.'

'Angela will fix you up. I've got to get back to my meeting. See you tonight. God, Ashley, I wish you wouldn't do things like this . . .'

He ambled off shaking his head.

So that was the kind of reception I got in London. By the time I left, I knew every corner of Dad's apartment. It was awesome in a glossy, magazine kinda way. All interior-designed with ankle-deep carpets and antiques everywhere. The furniture was all made in the kind of woodwork that shone with a gleam that said 'money'. Dad wasn't around much. He spent most of his time in Geneva or Tokyo or Brussels. But he saw that I had everything I needed – like the use of his chauffeur-driven limo if I wanted to go anywhere and a wadge of notes in my wallet every time it got empty. And of course everything was done for me by Conchita, the maid. She came in every day. In fact, I had everything I could wish for . . . I don't think I've ever been so lonely in my whole life.

So, one morning I got up and took a long hard look at myself in the mirror. My looks were the one and only asset I had. It was about time I capitalised on them. But this time I wasn't going to be half-hearted about it. If I was going to take modelling seriously, Man – I was heading right for the top. I was going to show Cherie that I could make it on my own.

That's when I found I had a few things to learn:

Number one: No-one wants to see a dumb book full of catalogue shots.

Number Two: Paying some guy £200 to take some decent shots of me was a rip-off – the shots were lousy.

Number Three: I was too young. Would you believe it? You read all this stuff about supermodels who've dropped straight out of kindergarten, but, when it comes to the actual point of giving you work, every-one is ultra-wary of booking you if you're under sixteen. So I fixed that one. I did a neat little forgery job on the birthdate in my passport – and *kapow* – I was seventeen overnight!

Actually, when it came to finding work, I discovered London was a pretty tough place. I think maybe I wasn't handling people right. All the English people I met, particularly in the fashion business, seemed really posey. They all had this hard stand-offish attitude, like being European made them extra special or something. I just talked straight back to them – like I wasn't going to be intimidated by anyone. And I really put their backs up – like they thought I was being too brash or too rude or just too American! I was starting to think like I couldn't get through to *anyone*.

That's until I met Chrissie. I met Chrissie at this agent's place – Marco Morandi's. She was the first English girl to be nice to me. It had been a pretty disastrous morning up till then. I had been turned down in a totally off-hand way by three different agencies and, to top it all (it was just *so* humiliating) – I *fell up Marco's stairs!* I was wearing these absolutely lethal platform-boots and I bust a heel. I practically bust my ankle, too – but that's when my luck started to change. I kind of limped into Marco's office feeling like Richard the Third on a bad day. I thought he'd just send me packing, but instead he made me sit down while he took a long hard look at me. Then he disappeared into a backroom and reappeared with this jar of cold-cream and some cotton-wool and told me to take all the junk off my face. And then, when I was reduced to sitting feeling like some freak with a dead naked face covered in cold-cream grease, he just roared with laughter at me, and said: 'Hey, what do you know? There's a beautiful girl underneath!'

It was through Marco I managed to get some pretty good test shots taken for my book. One of them was kinda weird 'cos I'd come out looking like I was made of ice or something – but that was the one that got me the Klavin casting. And that's what got me the Ange Bleu launch job – and *that's* why I'm here, sitting in a train going to Paris. Hey, I'm still having to pinch myself to see if I'm awake! Paris!

I've wanted to go to Paris ever since I was *born*, practically. The very word 'Paris' gives me delicious shivers all the way down my spine.

My train of thought was broken at this point by an announcement in English and then French telling us that we were about to enter the Tunnel. Suddenly everything outside went black. We were under the Channel and next thing I knew we were in France!

Hey! Eiffel Tower! Baguettes! Boulangeries! Maxim's! Moulin Rouge! Hey, Paris! Here I come!

Two

This may sound crazy, but I simply hadn't realised that France would be so *foreign*. I mean, directly you climb out of the train at the Gare du Nord there's all this French coming at you. French that is fast and fluent and not sounding one bit like those lessons I never attended to at school. I mean, back home you don't see that much point in French – sitting in a dumb classroom, way over the other side of the Atlantic, France seems so impossibly far away.

I hauled my cases to a trolley or, *pardonnez-moi*, a *caddie*. The caddie was securely chained up and all the instructions on how to unchain it were in French, too. So I gave up on that and continued up the platform like some bag-woman, dragging my cases behind me.

I was just casting around wondering where to find a taxi when this guy came up to me and said something in French.

'Pardon,' I said. 'Je ne parle pas français.' Which is the only complete French sentence I can say with confidence. Useful maybe, but limited.

He then put his fingers up to his lips and indicated drinking a cup of coffee.

'Café?' he said.

'No, I don't want a café, I want a taxi,' I said. He looked disappointed and pointed at a sign, shrugging his shoulders and walking off. These French men certainly were weird.

The word for 'Taxi' at any rate is international, so I joined the queue for those. Once inside my cab, I showed the address of the hotel the Paris agency had booked me into to the driver.

'Hotel Criston. Bien sur, Mademoiselle,' he said.

The cab sped off, straight into a massive traffic jam. Everyone was hooting and gesticulating but the cab man didn't seem fazed at all. Jammed in there like that gave me a chance to take stock of my surroundings. First impression? OK, it was the posters everywhere – featuring what I was soon to discover were the twin French obsessions: food and sex. Everywhere you looked there were pictures of scantily-clad women with shamelessly come-hither gazes, or similar shameless plates oozing oil, butter, cream – everything from mussels to chocolate mousse – in full colour, flaunting their calories at you.

Then, all of a sudden, we were out of the traffic jam and overtaking everything in sight on the inside at breakneck speed. I clung on as the cab thundered down the street over the cobbles.

All I could snatch were fleeting glimpses: shops with peeling facades . . . strange French lettering that hadn't changed since the last century . . . buildings in washed-out colours – terracotta, fading blues, zinc and grey – all so old and so *quaint* . . . olive-skinned street workers in baggy blue uniforms . . . wide tree-lined boulevards that looked like they'd been there forever . . . streets lined by pavement cafés . . . ultra-cool-looking people everywhere . . .

In fact, the whole world seemed to be taking time out to sit and look chic and French and sophis-ticated . . . It was all just so awesomely Parisian!

The cab swung round a great square and we passed a carousel of wooden horses going round full pelt. Then, all of a sudden, we were dipping down into a tunnel and then re-emerging into daylight on a road that skirted the Seine. Here was another Paris – history book stuff – all heavy, medieval and silent. Below, over the slow-moving river, trees leaned towards their grey-green reflections. Above, stone-work cut like lace stood etched against the sky. And spanning the river was bridge after bridge – built to last forever – guarded by massive bronze statues, all standing in totally over-the-top heroic attitudes.

And then, as we swept along a boulevard, we passed a view that looked as if it had come straight off a tourist postcard, and I caught sight of something I recognised. OK, I'll admit it – it was the Eiffel Tower.

The cab slowed down as we arrived in a massive square with some sort of monumental column stand-ing right in the centre. As the driver came to a halt at the kerb he said: 'Voilà, Mademoiselle. L'Hotel Criston.'

I stepped out. Carpet ran across the sidewalk to where the taxi had stopped. A uniformed porter took charge of my luggage and it was whisked out of sight. Having paid the driver, I made my way across to the Reception area. The floors were marble-polished to a mirror finish, and the walls and ceiling had gold-embossed panelling covered with scenes full of naked cupids and garlands of flowers and stuff. It all looked to me like a totally OTT Hollywood movie set.

'You have a reservation, Mademoiselle?' Relief, relief – the girl on the Reception Desk spoke English and reassured me that the Hotel was expecting me.

Another porter had taken charge of my key and I was shown to a room on the seventh floor. Right at the top. He raised the shutters and threw open the long windows. I stepped on to a balcony and – Oh, boy! – there was the most mind-blowing view. On every side roofs stretched away into the distance. Wherever there was a gap halfway big enough, a shining dome, or a spire, or some ancient church tower topped by a statue glinting gold in the sunlight pierced its way through. It was all built in that endless dreamy misted grey that says time and age. As I leaned on the balcony and drank it all in somewhere across the city a church clock chimed and a flock of whistling birds swept by in a great arc. I had arrived – this was Paris.

But I wasn't alone. A figure stood hunched over the adjoining balcony. There was something about the girl that was familiar. Then she turned and caught me staring at her.

Would you believe it? It was the girl from the train. The one who had jumped the line at Waterloo. Quel coincidence! And she had the room right next door to mine.

'Hi,' I said, quite spontaneously.

She frowned. 'Do I know you?' she asked. She had some sort of foreign accent – but not French.

'No, I guess not,' I replied to this very obvious put-down.

She sat down in a sun lounger with her back to me and, opening a magazine, seemed intent on reading it.

Huh! I thought. *Doesn't* she *really fancy herself?* Who did she take herself for – Madonna?

I turned and went back through the double doors and sat down crossly on the bed. I had really bad vibes from this encounter. The girl had totally put me off my stroke. A fine welcome to Paris, I must say.

But hey! This was a pretty gorgeous room, actually. It was all done in cream and gold with cute mock Louis XIV furniture like they have in those really posey mansions of Newport millionaires – really lush. There was a wildly gilt and marble bathroom and, just off it, a massive walk-in closet big enough to take a movie star's entire wardrobe. And then there was another door to what I thought was going to be another closet – but hey! This led into a massive sitting room with a cinema-sized TV and a mini-bar and acres of antique-looking carpet. Boy, wow! I was in a suite!

I went back into the bedroom feeling considerably cheered up. A check on the balcony revealed that my 'friendly neighbour' had gone inside. I unpacked my clothes and took a shower and called room service to get my outfit for the next day pressed. With all this done, I felt much better. I stretched out on the really cushy bed and stared out of the window. This was Paris . . . Paris! Why should I care about having a really uptight cow next door?

I had nothing urgent on the agenda until a 'rendezvous' at 10 am at the Klavin offices next day, when they were going to let me in on some kind of secret – all sounded rather mysterious. So what should I do first? I was thirsty for a start so I decided to venture out and try one of those pavement cafés.

A few doors down from the hotel I found a typical French Café-Brasserie set out with tiny tables and mock-cane chairs. It was mid-afternoon – 3.30. The café was pretty empty. I guessed that must be their slack time between the lunch people and the evening crowd. There was only an old guy in a corner reading a newspaper and myself and just one waiter to serve us, who was standing behind the bar polishing glasses.

'Bonjour,' he said as I walked in. He was young and quite dishy, in a dark, French kind of way.

I didn't trust my French accent at that point to come out with a decent 'Bonjour', so I went up to the bar and said:

'You speak English?'

'A leetle, yes.' He stared at me through eyes that looked suspiciously as if he thought I was a dumb tourist. But I wasn't going to let him get the better of me.

'Do you do Diet Coke?'

'We have Coca Lite.'

'OK . . . I'll be over there.' I indicated a seat that had a good view down the street.

I sat at the table and lit a cigarette. OK, I know I'm ruining my health. Mom would have a blue fit. But I only smoke the *occasional* one. The guy just went on polishing glasses. He was taking his time.

As I finished my cigarette, I glared at him. He smiled back. This was just so infuriating! Was he going to serve me or was he going in for a glass-polishing marathon first?

I got up and walked over to the bar: 'Are you going to bring me that Coke, or what?'

'Oh, I am sorry.' he said with elaborate politeness. 'You didn't say you would like a Coke. You just asked if we 'ad it.'

'Are you trying to be funny?'

'Not at all. One Coca Lite for the lady. Please sit down.'

I waited three or four minutes longer and he fiddled around behind the bar, taking forever. I was just about to complain again when he swept over to my table and presented my Coke with a flourish. It was in a tall glass with loads of ice, slices of orange and lemon, cherries, two cocktail umbrellas, and a couple of stuffed olives in it.

'You *are* trying to be funny.'

'Yes and you are laughing. No?'

'No,' I said, keeping a straight face with determination.

'You are new in Paris, I think,' said the guy, hovering while I took a sip.

'I just arrived.'

'In that case, welcome to Paris. And may I give you some advice?'

I shrugged. He had some nerve for a waiter.

'In Paris, when we come into a shop or a café or a restaurant, first we always say "Bonjour". Then, when we order, we say "s'il vous plait" . . .'

'Are you trying to teach me manners?' I cut in. These Parisians were *so* arrogant!

'Certainly not. I am trying to teach you *French*.' he said this with an irresistible smile and I could tell that he had been kind of teasing me all along.

'Don't you have anything better to do with your time?' I countered.

'At this moment, no. How could I?'

'Thought you might have a few more glasses to polish or something.'

'I would much rather stay and talk with you. If that is OK?'

We were interrupted by the arrival of a couple of large American women who were thrusting their way into the café fussing over which table to take.

'Do you do tea?' the first one demanded.

'Regular tea. With milk. *Fresh* milk?' added the second.

'S'il vous plait,' I whispered.

'Bravo!' He winked at me.

'I think you have something to do now,' I said.

'I think you're right.' He went off to find them a table that wasn't in the sun, wasn't in the draught, etc etc.

I sat and finished my Coke watching the people go by. You could tell at a glance who were the tourists and who were the Parisians. The tourists dressed like they were out to conquer Everest. Universally, they were in trainers tough enough for mountain passes and they had that kind of all-weather clothing that makes even the fittest person look like a badly-wrapped parcel. The Parisians on the other hand were all in designer-cut linen suits and the women all had perfect hair, but in casual un-girly styles. I had never seen so many stunning-looking people in one street at one time.

When I'd finished my Coke I decided I'd go for a wander to see what Paris had to offer. But first I had to go back to the hotel and change into some shoes I could safely walk in. Sounds dumb doesn't it? But I had this real problem with my ankle. OK, it was my own fault, ever since that really bad sprain in London, I'd just ignored it. The orthopaedic specialist I went to in the end said I was lucky not to have caused permanent damage. I had to sit with my leg up for a whole week. I nearly missed the Klavin casting – and I had to wear jeans for that because my leg was still black and blue. So now I had to exercise every day and be really careful because the ankle was still kind of weak.

Anyway, back at the hotel, when I picked up my key from Reception, the receptionist said: 'There is a message for you.'

It was from Visage – the Paris agency which had done the tie-up with my London Agency, Marco Morandi.

It was jotted down on a hotel slip – all written in French so I couldn't read it.

'Could you translate this for me?'

'Of course.' The receptionist glanced down the message.

'It says that a Monsieur Jacques Bernard will come here at 8.30 pm to take you both out to dinner.'

'Both?'

'Yes, it says "tous les deux". That is "both", is it not?'

I went up to my room wondering who on earth this mysterious other person could be. Maybe it was a mistake. The receptionist must have got it wrong.

I had time on my hands till the evening, so went for a long walk in this massive park. It was full of gravel walks and statues and fountains and these cute little green pagoda places where they sold soft drinks and salads and stuff. After walking for an hour or so, I sat down on one of the green tipped-back garden seats that were scattered about everywhere. The park was full of people intent on the serious business of enjoying themselves. And I thought how different it all was from New York or London where everyone seems to be hell-bent on being busy all the time.

And then I suddenly had this guilty thought that I shouldn't be sitting in the sun at all – no way was I allowed to get a tan – so I had to move into the shade. What it is to be a slave to your body!

Three

By seven that evening I was back in the hotel, soaking in a big tub full of bath-oil and wondering what to wear for dinner. There had been nothing in the message to indicate whether we were going to Maxim's or McDonald's. This was a tricky one. Still, this Monsieur Bernard was from Visage, and they were really top bookers . . . I simply had to impress him.

I climbed into the big white fluffy bathrobe that came courtesy of the hotel and started a full-scale assessment of my current clothing situation. Monsieur Jacques Bernard conjured up a picture of someone sophisticated and middle-aged with a hint of grey in his sideburns – I didn't want to look like some kid being taken out on a birthday treat. After trying on and rejecting about six different outfits (this is where I'd invested all that money Dad had given me in London), I settled on my most sophisticated black evening-dress. I hadn't even shown this one to Dad. He'd have freaked if he'd seen it. It was skin-tight with a massive slit up one side and had a kind of Madonna-like cone-shaped top that was really over-the-top sexy. I looked about thirty in it. I added a pair of shoes that had a wedge heel and tiny straps – and having gone this far I had to go the whole way. So I set to applying what Chrissie had called my 'wild-child' make-up. Here's how it goes on:

Firstly, the base – I blanked out my whole face to a matt pale creamy beige. I set all this with a dusting of matt translucent powder – applied with the softest and fluffiest of my brushes. Next, the eyes: I drew a rim of deep blue eye-pencil, just smudged ever so slightly to look soft and natural at the edges, and more powder to set this. I added some width and height with creamy-beige on the brow bone and deepened the eye-sockets with my favourite cool mauvey-blue. Now, mascara – ever so, ever so carefully applied – the lashes combed through whenever it threatened to clog. I redefined the cheekbones with a deep tea-rose blusher and ran a dusting of this under my chin. And, lastly the lips. I defined the shape with a deep scarlet lipliner and filled them in with a glossy pillar-box red, called Scarlett – my all-time favourite. The whole process took three-quarters of an hour precisely.

'Grrrrrrr . . .' I looked ferocious! Monsieur Bernard was going to have something to live up to!

I paced up and down my room for a while, testing out the shoes. I reckoned I could do quite a convincing entrance, I just hoped there wouldn't be a flight of stairs where we were going.

At 8.35 precisely I took the lift down to Reception. The lift doors opened and I looked around for a distinguished middle-aged man. There was no-one there but that uptight ego-tripper from the room next door to mine who was sitting with some young guy in jeans and a black leather jacket. Her boyfriend, I presumed.

I went over to the Reception Desk.

'I'm expecting a Monsieur Bernard.'

'Yes, Monsieur Bernard 'as arrived. 'Ee is over there,' said the girl.

I turned and at the same moment the guy in the black leather jacket got up and walked over to me.

'Ashe?' he asked, holding out a hand – he was older close up and had a face etched with smile lines – 'I'm Jack. Welcome to Paris.'

'But you're not French?'

'Only by adoption. I come from LA.'

I said, 'Hi, quel relief to meet a fellow American!'

The girl got up too. 'So, do you two know each other?' asked Jack. 'This is Ingrid. Ingrid Sandström. She's just over from London, too.'

'Hi,' I said. 'I guess we have already met. Kind of.'

Ingrid was busy taking in every detail of my appearance. She shook me by the hand with the strength of a Viking. She didn't have a touch of make-up on and she was wearing a loose mini-dress made of a dull grey linen and high-heeled canvas sandals. I have never felt so over-dressed in my life. I could feel myself going hot from embarrassment under my make-up. I just felt so, so brash.

'Look, maybe I should just change or something . . . I started.

'Change? Certainly not. You look wonderful!' said Jack. Ingrid didn't say anything.

Jack had a taxi standing outside and I noticed

Ingrid stood and waited for him to open the door for her. Then, when she climbed in, she didn't slide across the seat to make room for us or anything, she just sat there, so Jack and I had to walk around the other side and get in.

On the way to the restaurant, Jack, having discovered it was my first trip to Paris, played the polite host and pointed out the sights. We drove around the Place de la Concorde and up the Champs Elysées. At the top, cars came flying at us from all angles. Jack explained that Paris isn't built in a nice sensible grid like New York, but in loads of star shapes. It's like a game of 'chicken' at every intersection. That's why Parisian drivers are all maniacs.

Ingrid didn't say a word all the way to the restaurant. When we arrived she swept in first as if she wasn't with us. I felt as if this was pretty much my fault. The place was packed with people who were really stylish in an understated way. In my totally over-the-top dress, I was causing quite a stir. And, as luck would have it, our table had to be right the way through the restaurant, didn't it? A waiter led us out on to an enormous open terrace that had the most fantastic view of the Eiffel Tower. As we wound our way through the crowded tables absolutely *everyone* turned to look at me. I could happily have sunk through the earth.

But Jack didn't seem to mind a bit. In fact I think he was rather enjoying it. As we sat down, he whispered, 'I wonder what's wrong with that guy over there?'

'What guy, where?'

He pointed out a really grossly enormous man in the corner of the restaurant. He was studying the menu with concentration.

'He's the only guy who didn't stare when you came in. But maybe he's more interested in the food.'

I hoped Ingrid hadn't heard. To tell you the truth all this attention was really embarrassing. At that moment I would have given anything to look totally cool and casual like her.

Jack was ordering drinks. Ingrid asked for a Campari Soda and I ordered a Coca Lite.

'You don't drink?' asked Jack.

I shook my head.

'Very wise,' he said.

'How old are you?' asked Ingrid with a suddenness that caught me off-guard.

'Fift . . . I mean seventeen,' I said.

'I thought so.' She raised an eyebrow and smiled at Jack. I wasn't going to stand for this.

'And how old are you?' I countered.

'Twenty-three,' she said.

'And I am a poor old man of thirty-five,' said Jack pulling a sad face, obviously trying to defuse the atmosphere. 'So, now we have our ages sorted out, what are we going to eat?'

The menu was in absolutely unintelligible French so I ordered the only things I could reliably recognise, which was 'bifsteak et salade verte'.

While we waited for our food to arrive Jack bombarded me with questions about places he knew in New York – whether they were still there and whether people went there any more. Ingrid just sipped her drink in silence and I started to feel awkward about the fact that she was being left out of the conversation. So I turned to her and said: 'New York's OK – but I just *love* Paris, don't you? I mean look at it . . .' I turned towards the Eiffel Tower floodlit against the night sky. It looked like it was putting on a show just for us with the lights of the city glittering all around it. 'Ever since I was a little kid it's always been my dream to come here. I can hardly believe it's come true.'

Ingrid was unimpressed. She just said in her doleful Swedish accent: 'Yes it is picturesque, I suppose. But personally I prefer Milan. The people there have more style.'

'Well, I've never been to Milan. I've only ever been to London and Paris apart from home, and I just feel on an all-time high. It's just so awesome! And another thing – people don't just walk over you like they do in New York. You know at the station today when I arrived, I was just standing around looking lost trying to find a cab and this guy came up and asked if I wanted a cup of coffee. Must've thought I was looking for the station bar. I mean you'd never get that in New York . . .'

Jack choked on his Martini at that point. He seemed to think what I had said was terribly funny for some reason.

'He was trying to pick you up,' said Ingrid staring at me as if I was the dumbest thing on two legs.

'That's the standard Parisian chat-up line,' said Jack: ' "Would you like a coffee?" means "I like the look of you".'

'Oh, I see,' I said, feeling really foolish.

We were interrupted by the arrival of our food. Ingrid's order was a plate of pancakes with a creamy cheese sauce and after that she'd ordered ravioli. I wondered how she kept that bean-thin figure of hers. Actually, I have to be pretty careful about what I eat. I mean, Mom's strict training like 'no ice-cream, no French fries, no candy' had really paid off and I was generally pretty slim. But go mad and I could easily put on a few pounds and those really showed in front of the camera. But Ingrid was slim as anything. Almost unnaturally so.

'Goodness, Ingrid, you're so skinny! Lucky you, I guess you never have to worry about your weight,' I said, trying valiantly to break the ice again.

She shrugged. 'Guess I'm lucky in some things.'

Jack was drawing our attention to someone on the far side of the room. It was a guy with receding slicked-back hair and designer stubble wearing a baggy Armani suit. 'Look, it's Julio Iononi – and do you see who he's with?'

I looked over and recognised his face immediately. He'd dropped into the Klavin casting in London. I hadn't known who he was at the time. I'd been to so many castings they'd all kind of merged into a blur. He was with a middle-aged woman who had stunning broad cheekbones and a massive mouth. Her face was familiar as well, but I couldn't place who she was.

'That's Juliette Romano – she was one of the big stars of those old Seventies Antonioni films. Julio knows simply everyone,' said Jack. 'In spite of his big reputation in the film world, he's a regular guy. His English is a bit original, and so are some of his friends, but I think he's gonna just love you, Ashe.'

Ingrid got up at this point and went to the Ladies' Room. So the two of us were left alone.

'Uh uh,' said Jack. 'I think I well and truly put my foot in it that time.'

'What do you mean?'

'Miss Strong-and-Silent isn't best pleased.'

'I don't understand why she's being such a drag,' I said. 'I mean, it's a lovely evening, a fabulous place. Yet she's sitting here like she's at a wake or something.'

'I knew it would be a mistake to put you two together.'

'What do you mean?'

'The Ange Bleu launch, maybe you didn't know? She was up for it too . . . But you got it.'

'I had no idea.'

'She was offered stand-in, and she nearly hit the roof. She's been one of Klavin's favourites for as long as anyone can remember. Surely you must recognise her?'

I shook my head.

'The girl who appears semi-naked, swathed in Klavin belts?

'That's Ingrid?'

Jack nodded.

'But she wasn't half so skinny then,' I pointed out. 'She looked absolutely fantastic, in fact. What's happened to her?'

'Who knows? She's doing mainly catwalk now.

She's here for the Collections. But she's being pretty unprofessional if you ask me. She may be pissed off about not getting the launch, but that's life. It happens all the time. She should be able to rise above it.'

When Ingrid came back she looked as if she'd been crying.

'I hear you're here for the Collections,' I said. 'It must be a really fun time, all those parties and . . .'

She gave me condescending look. 'You've never done catwalk?'

I shook my head. 'No, but I'd love to.'

'Fun?' said Ingrid. 'It's a meat-market. If you're doing the circuit – London, Milan, Paris, New York – your main object is not to get sick. Half the time you're so exhausted you can hardly stand up on your feet. You don't even get time to eat. Parties? You must be kidding. While the shows are on, they're the last thing on your mind.'

The meal continued with further attempts by us to defrost a little of Ingrid's icy mood. Jack entertained us by picking out the celebrities in the restaurant and giving us the lowdown on them.

'And *he's* a government minister, the girl with him is not his wife – or his daughter, either,' he said with a grin. 'And that blonde over there, she's not a she, but a he.'

'Really!' I said, trying not to stare. 'She' looked really convincing. Paris was quite an eye-opener.

But it was pretty much a waste of time trying to inject life into Ingrid, she just looked bored out of her mind. By the time we were on to the coffees, I

31

was looking forward to getting back to the hotel and to bed. I had to get an early night because of the Klavin rendezvous next day. Then, just as we were about to leave, Ingrid got up and disappeared to the loo again. That was the third time.

While we were waiting, Julio Iononi came past our table, and paused to talk to Jack, so Jack introduced us.

I held out my hand to shake hands: 'Do you remember me? From the casting?'

'But of course . . .' he said, and he leaned down and kissed my hand instead of shaking it. Very old-time, very Continental! 'Until Tuesday,' he said. 'And then no more nights out. We start to *work*.' And he gave a mock-serious frown.

Ingrid had been gone ages. Jack kept looking at his watch.

'Maybe you ought to go and check if she's still alive.'

In the Ladies I heard someone furiously flushing the loo and then Ingrid emerged from a cubicle looking red-eyed.

'Say, are you OK?' I asked.

'Fine. Why do you ask?' she snapped.

'I'm sorry I did,' I countered. Boy, she was touchy.

Anyway, in spite of Ingrid, it had been a pretty fantastic evening. My first evening in Paris. I went to sleep that night thinking that, of all the people in the world, I must be pretty much the all-time luckiest.

Four

Klaus Klavin's offices were in the rue St Honoré. I got up early that morning and washed my hair and then, once I'd dried it, I went the whole hog and put heated rollers in. I checked every detail of my appearance twice over. I even did my nails twice and sat and let the varnish dry for a full ten minutes. And I rubbed masses of handcream in to make my hands look really smooth. When you're a model even the tiniest detail can get noticed and commented on.

Make-up for the day was going to be minimal, I'd learned my lesson the night before. And the dress I had selected to wear was plain cream linen, couldn't have been simpler. Lou-Lou, who is my booker at Marco Morandi's, had warned me about Paris. She said if I even so much as went into a shop in the rue St Honoré in jeans and sneakers I'd get treated like dirt.

She'd given me a thorough briefing. Originally, I had imagined if I went to the Klaus Klavin offices, I'd actually meet him. But apparently he was far too rarified to work in an office. Klavin was an empire and Klaus Klavin himself had tiers and tiers of people under him who actually did the work. Pretty well nobody ever saw the man himself. It was like he was God or something.

The person I had to see this morning was Emile Maréchal, the Paris Marketing Director of Klavin Products. He had a reputation for being a really tough guy. So I was going to the Klavin offices prepared to be on my best behaviour.

Anyway, I emerged from the hotel looking, by my standards, pretty damn perfect, and got the doorman to wave down a cab for me.

'Klaus Klavin, 229 rue St Honoré,' I said to the driver.

The driver shrugged and shook his head and gesticulated towards the corner of the square. He seemed to be flatly refusing to take me there. This was totally out of line.

The doorman who was listening in, said: ' 'Ee says, 'ee cannot drive you there – 'ees not far enough.' And he pointed to a building on the corner of the square. ' 'Ees there.' He was right. I could just make out the Klaus Klavin logo, a subtle gold on the facade.

It was all of a hundred yards away. I felt a real airhead as I walked the tiny distance to their door.

The Klavin showrooms had a window decorated with six transparent Perspex models wearing nothing but Klavin dark glasses and black leather belts with Klavin logo buckles.

As I pushed open the crystal-clear glass doors, I noticed that even the door handles were modelled like Klavin perfume bottle tops. Cool eh? Cool was the word – inside was air-conditioned and everything was icily perfect. The room breathed a kind of Klaus Klavin aura. Crystal-clear showcases finished in the house colours of gloss-black, gold, sapphire and beige displayed single items from the Klavin designer range as if they were museum pieces.

An assistant wearing a geometrically cut Klavin suit came forward to meet me.

'Puis-je vous aider, Madame?'

'Do you speak English?'

'But of course, naturally.'

'I have an appointment to see Monsieur Emile Maréchal at 10.30.'

She took my name and led me through the boutique to an atrium lined with weird exotic plants. In the centre, a futuristic lift, made entirely out of clear Perspex, stood waiting. I was directed to the sixth floor and the lift silently glided, like a clear plastic bubble with me in it, to the top. It was just like being in a sci-fi movie.

At the sixth floor the lift opened on to acres of Klavin beige carpet. A pair of faultless tanned Parisian legs were making their way towards me.

'Miss Garnett? Please follow me.'

I was led to an icy air-conditioned conference room. It seemed that as well as the honour of being presented to Monsieur Maréchal, a Monsieur Monard, who was in charge of Research and Development, was there to meet me too.

Both men were wearing baggy Klavin suits and ties in the Klaus Klavin colours. It was as if they were all in a uniform or something. At that thought I was tempted to giggle. But I subdued the impulse.

Everything in the Klavin offices was icily cool and deadly, deadly serious.

I shook hands in a suitably formal way and then Monsieur Monard said he was going to 'present' the Ange Bleu 'flask' to me. He sat with his hand on this box on the conference table, as if it held a priceless relic. He then went on at length telling me what a highly-favoured person I was to be allowed to see inside this magic box of his. And that I would have to be sworn to secrecy not to tell a soul about what I had seen until after the Ange Bleu Press Launch. Quel fuss! It was only a silly old perfume bottle for goodness sake. I was starting to feel as if I was being recruited by the CIA.

He droned on about this old bottle of his, being the result of three years' creative development and loads and loads of consumer research and that all this had been done in deadly secrecy. Then, at last, he looked as if he was going to open it up.

He leaned forward and said: 'So you can be trusted, yes?'

I nodded. 'Cross my heart and hope to die.'

Monsieur Maréchal nodded to Monsieur Monard. He opened the box with a flourish.

Inside, resting on cushioned blue velvet, was a perfume bottle. It looked as if it had been sculpted out of crystal. It was in the shape of a female figure striding forward in flowing robes.

'May I touch?'

He nodded. 'Take it.'

'Do you know the statue *Victoire de Samothrace*?' he asked. 'The English call it *Winged Victory*.'

I shook my head. I felt really dumb. I had no idea what he was talking about.

'It is probably the most famous statue in the world. And it is the inspiration for Ange Bleu.'

'And see what happens when it has perfume in it.' He swung the presentation case around and took out a second bottle, this time filled with pale blue liquid.

I'd never seen blue perfume before. As he turned the bottle, the blue refracted through the rippled glass, giving an effect of shimmering movement.

'Perhaps it is not what you expect from Klaus Klavin?' he said.

'No, definitely not.'

'You see, with "K" and "Klavinesse" Klavin holds the number one and number two positions in the perfume market. This success gives us special problems. Each time we introduce a perfume, we do not wish our customers to simply switch to the new one – that way we don't gain anything. We call this in marketing, "cannibalisation".'

'You mean, like people eating people?'

'Like eating into our own profit.'

'I see.'

'So our strategy is to create a perfume that people who have never bought a Klavin perfume before will want to buy.'

'You make it sound like some kind of war.'

'It is. It's a battle we have to fight to keep factories open. And to keep the jobs on which thousands of our employees depend. It is a war in a way.'

'I'd never thought about it like that.'

Monsieur Maréchal leaned forward and spoke for the first time: 'So what about our Blue Angel, herself. What do *you* think of the bottle?'

'I think it's awesome.'

He laughed: 'Awesome, eh? But would it make you buy our perfume? All our "boring" marketing talk won't sell a single bottle if young women like you don't like it.'

'It wasn't boring, actually. I didn't realise that so much went on behind the scenes.'

'What do you think we all do in these big offices?'

'I'd never really thought about it.'

'Don't,' he said. 'It's all very, very tedious!' and he smiled and patted me on the shoulder and said: 'Big secret, eh. Cross your heart and hope to die, eh?' and he chuckled.

He wasn't fierce at all. He was a real pussy-cat.

As I left the Klaus Klavin offices, I was feeling kind of thoughtful. I mean, I'd always been given all this hassle from politically-correct-type people about modelling. About being part of the whole advertising scene that was kind of bent on corrupting people. Like it was forcing them to buy stuff they didn't really need. Nobody had ever put forward the other side of the argument. Like it was all part of keeping factories going and keeping people in work. But on the other hand, no-one really *needs* perfume do they? It was kind of like a conundrum I couldn't solve.

A few blocks down, I caught sight of the café where that jumped-up French waiter worked. I didn't have anything to do until the shoot started next morning and was wondering how to spend the afternoon. Hey, maybe now I was all dressed up and looking cool, I'd go in there and give that guy a hard time. He needed taking down a peg or two.

I strode in.

He was behind the bar polishing glasses again.

As I walked in, I was rewarded by seeing that he kind of stared and then did a double-take as he recognised me.

I could see from the mirrors on the walls I was looking pretty good, as a matter of fact. This time he stopped what he was doing immediately and grabbed a tray and came over to where I was sitting. And hey! I caught him just sneaking a glance at himself in the mirror and smoothing his hair back. Guys! I reckon they're just about twice as vain as we are.

'Bon jour,' I said teasingly with narrowed eyes, as he arrived at my table.

He shook his head.

'Uh uh – it is not bon jour but bon*jour*,' he said, putting the emphasis on the second syllable.

'Bon*jour*,' I tried again. He made me say it three times before he was satisfied.

'Better,' he said. 'Not perfect, but better,'

'Je veux un Coca Lite, s'il vous plait,' I said, mustering just about all the French I could remember.

'Excellent,' he said. 'Now try "Je voudrais un Coca Lite, s'il vous plait." That is even better.'

'What's better about it?'

'It is, how you say, more polite.'

'You *are* trying to teach me manners.'

'No, I would not dream of it. I am trying to teach

you *French...*' I still couldn't really tell if he was joking or not.

'Well, do I get to have a drink or not? A girl could die of thirst over here before she's learned how to order.'

He came back with a big glass of Coke with loads of ice and kind of hovered.

'Merci,' I said.

'So, you do speak French.'

'A leetle,' I said imitating his accent.

'What you need is practice. Perhaps even your very own French professeur.'

'Oh, yes, sure. Maybe you could suggest someone?'

'Well, my French is superb actually. I am speaking it all my life.'

'It's a generous offer.'

'Of course, I would need something in return.'

'Uh huh?' I thought so. 'Like what?'

'The truth is, I would like to photograph you.'

'If you want to photograph me, you can talk to my agent. My rate is currently around two hundred dollars an hour.' I guessed that should put him in his place.

'That's a pity,' he said, frowning.

'Yeah, well, I kind of thought it might be a problem.'

'You see, I hoped we could make, how you say, "a straight swop"?' He paused. 'For teaching you French I would have to charge a lot more than that.'

The cheek of it! I had to laugh at that. He laughed too. You know, he had a simply knockout smile.

'OK, it's a deal!' I held out my hand. 'You get one shot at a picture for every French sentence you can teach me.'

He shook my hand looking serious. 'A straight business deal, as you say.'

Then it suddenly occurred to me to ask: 'Say, have you ever heard of a statue called *something* of Samothrace?'

'*Victoire de Samothrace* – naturally. Everyone has heard of the *Victoire*. It's in the Louvre.'

'Can just anyone go and see it?'

'Of course, but the Louvre is very big. There are many different galleries. The statue is so difficult to find. Americans have been known to be lost for days in there. Some never come out alive.'

'Really?'

'You need someone who knows their way around to guide you. It's like how do you say – a *labarinthe*.'

'A labyrinth?'

'Yes.'

'I see.'

There was a pause.

'Do you know many people in Paris?' he asked.

I shook my head.

He glanced at his watch.

'Of course, I could, if you like, go with you. I stop working at four o'clock. I could maybe spare the time.' He sneaked a glance at me.

He was trying to pick me up. I could tell. Here was me, kind of like the all-time star of a top-class perfume launch, being picked up by a waiter. But actually, he *was* kind of cute. We were only going to an art gallery. So why not?

'OK, you're on,' I said. 'I just gotta get back to the hotel and change first.'

'Outside here at four, then,' he said.

I was back outside the café at 4.15. My waiter, now transformed out of his uniform of shiny black trousers, waistcoat and apron, into a normal-looking (actually a drop-dead gorgeous) French boy in worn blue jeans and a polo-neck, was waiting on the corner, smoking a cigarette.

'We can get a cab outside my hotel,' I said, pointing towards the Criston.

'Is that where you stay?' he asked. He looked impressed.

'Yeah, it's no big deal. I'm not picking up the tab.'

'What is this thing – this "tab"?'

'The bill,' I explained and then added teasingly: 'The 'ow-you-say – l'addition?'

'OK, so who is?'

'Some people I'm working for.'

He nodded but didn't enquire further.

'We do not need a taxi,' he said. 'Paris is small. It is best always to walk. And you see more, too.'

I was glad I'd put on my trainers. Actually, after all the fuss of the morning it was great to be walking along in jeans and a T-shirt – the two of us just looking like any other ordinary guy and girl out together in the city.

We walked across the Place de la Concorde and then under an underpass that led down to the Seine.

On the way we established that his name was Sasha and mine was Ashe – and I told him a bit about how I'd come over from New York to do some modelling. I guess, I was laying it on a bit. Well, who wouldn't? But he made a real effort not to look over-impressed.

The footpath we were walking on was along the embankment of the Seine, almost at water level – it was that famous one that features in all those corny old French movies you see on late night TV – where lovers sit on benches and snog and stuff.

Actually, it made me kind of think – I hadn't had a boyfriend in ages. No-one since Logan, and that had been just one big disaster. Logan went to my High School, he was two years above me, so to start with I was kind of flattered that he noticed me. And then, once we were going out together, he got really possessive. I mean, he wouldn't let me so much as *look* at another boy. It was like we were married or something. If I so much as talked to anything vaguely masculine he'd go all hang-dog and make me feel real bad about it. Logan was another big reason why I left New York, as a matter of fact. I just couldn't take the guilt-trips he kept sending me on. But now, being on my own for this long, I was kind of missing having a guy around.

I cast a sideways glance at Sasha. He was really yummy actually, in a French way that was different from the boys back home. He was lean and strong with gorgeous green eyes. I caught myself wondering if he had a girlfriend.

We arrived at the Louvre just in time to go in with the very last group. Actually, the building alone was pretty gasp-worthy. Sasha explained that it was built as a royal palace and it must have been for some all-time powerful king because the place was

43

gi-normous. There were just endless vistas of golden creamy-coloured stone with masses of pillars and fussy carving and statues all over the place.

And then, plonked down slap in the middle of this vast open courtyard with all this fancy old stuff round the sides, was this amazing ultra-modern glass pyramid. There were loads of people my age milling around the pyramid. Some had guide books or sketch pads and mostly they looked as if they were into all this culture stuff in a big way. Personally, I don't really go in for art much. I'd been to MoMA once with Cherie, but she'd got talking to this guy she met in the lobby and then we'd spent most of the time with him in the coffee shop.

Anyway, Sasha pretty much seemed to know his way around. He led the way down the moving staircase that went right under the pyramid and he knew just which gallery the statue was in, without having to ask anyone. He insisted on buying our tickets to go in, which was kind of nice but embarrassing too, considering how loaded I was.

The Louvre was absolutely jam-packed with tourists. I followed Sasha as he dodged between different groups of these dedicated culture-seekers. They were all in keen little huddles, bunched around their guides. As we passed we could catch a running commentary that switched from German to Spanish to Italian to Japanese depending on the cut of their leisure-wear. Each huddle was craning up at walls which were covered with big stagey paintings.

The first few galleries were full of massive gods battling their way through clouds and giant warriors chopping each other's heads off. Then there were all these scantily-clad goddesses, kind of trying to cover themselves up and not being too good at it. There was one semi-naked lady in particular, who stared down in a kind of horrified amazement at seeing all these tourists ogling her.

As we paused in front of her painting, which was a particularly lavish scene full of cherubs and chariots, and huge flying people in robes, I said to Sasha: 'Don't you find all this stuff kind of *showy* compared with modern stuff?'

He nodded. 'It's like a big cinema screen, isn't it? Imagine what it must have been like to look at pictures like this, before cinema, before television, before photographs, even. This is by Rubens. Brilliant, isn't it?'

Actually I wasn't so wild about all this over-the-top complicated stuff so I said: 'So how come *you* know so much about art?'

'For a waiter, you mean?'

I looked away. He had read my mind, I hadn't meant to sound so condescending.

'Actually, I have a confession to make. I'm not a real waiter. I'm a photographer. Or trying to be. I just work at the café to make money.'

So that's why he wanted to photograph me. He was after some classy shots for his portfolio. It wasn't *me* he was interested in.

'OK. So how come a photographer knows so much about art?'

'Photography is about looking – about the pleasure of looking at beautiful things . . .'

'Like paintings?'

'And people . . .' He cast a sideways glance at me.

Maybe this was a compliment, I couldn't be sure. Anyway, I wasn't going to acknowledge it. So I pointed out the particularly gross fat female who was being so totally inefficient in holding up her drapes.

'Like her for instance?'

'I think perhaps she was very beautiful for a woman of her time. Personally, I prefer girls a little larger,' he said with a grin.

After that we had a sort of jokey competition searching through the paintings to see if we could find a female big enough to suit him and then suddenly we were out of the galleries and in a long, cool stone room full of statues that led to a wide flight of stone steps.

'There it is,' said Sasha. 'Your statue – *Victoire de Samothrace*.'

In the darkness of the gallery the statue was caught in a shaft of golden light – and, although obviously carved out of stone, this gave it an eerie effect of weightlessness. The figure seemed to hover above its rough stone plinth.

I could see immediately how this had inspired the Ange Bleu bottle. It was a female figure, and although it had, at some point in the past, lost its arms and head, you could tell it was the body of an all-time knockout woman. You could trace the shape of her body striding in a purposeful way through her billowing robes. The whole statue seemed to be about to take off into the air.

We came closer and I read the inscription below it:

' "Vers 190 av. J.C." What does that mean?'

'One hundred and ninety years before Jesus Christ. The statue is over two thousand years old.'

'Boy – you know, I don't think I've ever seen anything that old.'

'Maybe not – not in America.'

'You know what's weird about it? It's like it's moving, yet it's standing still.'

We just stood and looked at it for some minutes. It made me kinda stop and think – to realise someone, so long ago, could have done that. Could have carved movement like that into solid rock – it was really something, you know.

A bell sounded at that point and one of the uniformed attendants started ushering people towards the doors. It seemed the gallery was about to close.

We didn't talk much on the way out. It was odd – I mean, I've never really rated art much. I'd always considered people who went on and on about it as kind of pseuds or poseurs, just out to create a big impression and prove to you just how cultured they were. But this statue had really got to me. For just one moment I had understood what all the fuss was about.

It had been really hot in the Louvre and I was gasping for a drink.

'I'm thirsty. Can I buy you a drink? How about over there?' I could just see a café on the far side of the square.

'The Café Marly – it is very – er, stylish.' I could tell he meant expensive.

'That's no problem. So are we,' I said.

'You are right. Let's go there.'

It was a pretty smart café actually. We were shown on to a long terrace with groups of tables and chairs overlooking the pyramid. As we chose a table, I caught sight of a figure I recognised.

'Hey, look. There's Julio Iononi,' I whispered.

Julio turned at that point and caught sight of me. He lifted his glass and smiled and waved. I felt really flattered, actually.

'Do you know him?' asked Sasha.

'I'm in the commercial he's here to shoot. We start tomorrow.'

It was good to see Sasha's jaw positively drop. 'You are working with Julio Iononi?'

I nodded and tried to look really matter-of-fact. 'Sure, why?'

'But he's brilliant. I love his work. The man's a genius.'

I shrugged. 'I sure hope so.'

Five

My wake-up call the next morning was at 5 am. A taxi was coming for me at six and by then I was meant to have showered and washed and dried my hair and eaten a nourishing breakfast that would last me through to lunchtime. I gulped down muesli and a black coffee in bed and had an apple while I was in the shower.

The filming was to be in two separate sections. I'd been taken through all this in London when I got the part. There were sequences that were to be shot in a studio, in which I was to be the spirit of Ange Bleu and there were real-life shots on location which were to come later. The final commercial was going to have shots of me as a typical Parisian girl living a city life, intercut with the Ange Bleu shots. The idea behind the commercial was kind of – surreal – like every time this real-life me passes someone and they get a waft of the perfume, I'm meant to morph into the Ange Bleu. I had to ask what 'morph' meant. It's a technique which turns one image on film into something else – like turning Michael Jackson into a panther, for instance. They switch from one image to the other by computer-animating all the stages in between. The whole idea of the commercial sounded weird to me, but I guessed Iononi knew what he was doing.

Anyway for the Ange Bleu shots all I was going to have to do was pose in a wind tunnel. Didn't sound too challenging, did it?

The taxi that came to collect me seemed to drive forever. We eventually arrived, miles outside Paris, at this kind of airstrip in the middle of a vast industrial estate where there was a hangar in which they tested aircraft. The Production Company had hired a commercial air tunnel for the day. I felt very small and insignificant as I made my way towards this massive building. In between odd lost-looking bits of aircraft, like tail-fins and stuff, I spotted the usual paraphernalia of a shoot. Trucks with generators throbbing and cables slithering out of them were lined up outside. There were the technical vans with engineers in earphones milling around. And the usual big mobile catering unit. Already the scene was a hive of activity.

Once inside the hangar, I found the stylist and the make-up girl had improvised a cosy little corner for themselves and they were already setting up their gear. A runner was handing out coffees in Styrofoam cups.

The stylist was Italian but she spoke pretty good English and she had two assistants to help her.

'We will take hours to get you ready,' she said. 'I would not drink anything if I were you.' She had a load of sponges and a big cake of stuff that looked like a block of blue soap.

First I had to put on a virtually transparent body stocking and then I had to stand while they applied white base all over my body with a sponge. Not a pleasant experience! Once this had dried, they sponged this blue pigment stuff over the top, every bit of me had to be covered, except my face and arms. It dried into a strangely iridescent blue coating. This is when I realised what she'd meant about drinking. There was no way I'd be able to get out of the body stocking without ruining all their work.

Next they set to work on my face. This was blanked out with white, too, and then sculpted with a mauve-grey blusher along the cheekbones and jawline to give a carved, stone-like effect. The make-up girl deepened my eye-sockets with blue and gave me white highlights on the brow-bones. Next she used masses of deep steel grey eyeliner and then blanked out my lashes with white so that they disappeared and my eyelids looked like they were made of stone. Looking in the mirror, it was almost as if the missing head of the statue was being brought back into existence before my eyes. Weird.

Once I was made up, the stylist brought over the robe. There seemed to be several square miles of it – made of the finest grey silk chiffon. She slipped it over my head and it settled around my body as light as a cobweb. It felt like wearing nothing at all.

At that moment we heard a limousine draw up and there was a big commotion outside. Julio Iononi had arrived. Suddenly the film crew, who had been pretty much doing nothing, lounging around smoking and stuff, were galvanised into action. The make-up girls did a lightning clean-up and dusted down a chair for him.

As he came into the room the stylist stood back, nervously waiting for his approval. He sat in the chair and stared. And then he got up and walked around me, adjusting the dress here and there and turning my head from side to side.

'Move,' he said to me, looking stern.

I walked a few steps.

'Turn,' he commanded, still with his brows knitted.

And then his fact burst into a smile: 'Bellissimo,' he said and turned and hugged the stylist.

The actual shoot was just one big nightmare. Don't know if I mentioned I was scared of heights? My one big fear has always been being forced to go up the Empire State – and I'd steered pretty well clear of the Eiffel Tower ever since I'd been in Paris. Well, I'm telling you, this shoot was tailor-made to scare me rigid. I had to get into one of those hoist things like they have to mend streetlights and stuff. But, wait for it – they'd taken the safety rails off!! OK, so I was kind of strapped to a post like I was about to be burned at the stake or something – so I couldn't actually *fall* off. But try telling that to yourself as you're being raised a zillion yards off the ground.

One of Julio's assistants was in a similar hoist and he was taking Polaroids of me like there was no tomorrow. Then someone shouted something in French from below and a great fog of dry ice puffed up round me. So I wasn't just shaking from fear but from cold, too. Then – just as I decided that this was the ultimate in torture – the wind machine was started up. So there I was, pinned like a lolly to a stick, being turned into ice by what felt like a kind of freeze-drying process.

After about ten minutes of this I was brought down to earth again. One of the make-up girls came over to check my make-up.

'You OK?'

I shook my head. I was shivering. She ran off and fetched a blanket and the other girl got me a hot coffee. To hell with the body stocking, I was in need of the caffeine. While I was wrapped in the blanket sipping my coffee, Julio Iononi walked over:

'You have cold. Yes?'

I shook my head. 'It's OK . . . It's nothing. I'm fine now.'

'Five minutes . . . then we start again,' he said. 'You sure you are OK?'

I grinned back. 'No problem.'

'Good girl.'

Once I was on the hoist again I just tried to pretend I was down on the ground. I kept telling myself like Mom always said: 'Pain is all in the mind, Baby', 'Rise above it' and 'If it's not hurting, it's not working'. I pretended the wind was warm water. I forced myself to imagine that I was floating through warm water. It was warm. It was all around me. I could make it feel warm. I could do it. I could do anything.

The shoot went on for almost an hour. They had to take footage from every angle. Above, below, close-up, far away, you name it.

When at last I was down at ground level again,

Julio Iononi came up to me. He showed me one of the Polaroids.

'Is good, yes? Very strong.'

I nodded. Even though the Polaroid was of a pretty pathetic quality, I could see the effect he was trying to achieve. I looked unreal – like the statue had come to life and was striding through the wind.

'Thank you,' he said and he patted my shoulder. 'But you are like ice!'

'No, I'm fine really.'

'Very strong girl . . .' he said, nodding.

I shrugged. 'Guess I've had to be.'

He nodded approval and went off to talk to the technical crew.

We did three more takes after that. By the end of the day I guess I pretty much knew what cryonic suspension would feel like.

It took forever to get the make-up off. At 8 pm, I was back at the hotel, luxuriating in a deep tub of hot water and topping it up whenever it cooled down. I was scrubbing off the last vestiges of the iridescent blue when the phone rang. I reached out of the tub. Yes, there was even a phone in the bathroom, cool, huh?

It was Chrissie. You know, the girl I told you about – who's also with Morandi.

'Hi. How you doing?'

'You back from Australia?'

'I just flew in. Had to do this state-by-state promotional tour for U&U. I'm dead beat. How's it going with you?'

'If I survive today, I can survive anything.' I

gave her a quick rundown of my day.

She made sympathetic noises.

'When are you getting back to London?'

'In about a fortnight. Why?'

'Marco's giving a really big party for me. To celebrate the U&U campaign going worldwide.'

(Chrissie had been picked out of literally thousands to represent U&U jeans. She's dead skinny and has got legs up to her armpits. And she's really, really unaffected by looking so stunning.)

'Does that mean we're going to have to put up with seeing that great big butt of yours everywhere we look?'

'Yep, they've got me twenty yards high on all the hoardings. Not me alone, of course, there's Shane too.'

'He still addicted to mirrors?'

Chrissie giggled. 'He had his twenty-first last week – right in the middle of the tour. I gave him a really massive bottle of l'Egoïste aftershave, the biggest you can buy. I don't think he saw the irony of it, though.'

'Gee. I wish you were over here. All there is, is this skinny cow next door who's really got it in for me.'

'Who's that?'

'Miss Ingrid Gloom-and-Doom Sandström.'

'Ingrid Sandström? But she's really famous.'

'And doesn't she know it?'

'You must have made *some* friends.'

'Oh, there's this waiter in the café next door. He's actually studying photography. He's kind of cute.'

'Uh huh? Tell me more . . .'

'Not much more to tell. When's the party?'

She gave me the date. 'You'll get a proper invitation, of course. You've got to be there. Promise you'll try?'

I promised and then she started giving me the low-down on some of the other people at the agency.

'Hey, have you heard about Zoë? She's thinking of chucking in modelling.'

'But she's doing really well.'

'Marco's trying to talk her round.'

'Is she coming to the party?'

'Yes, and so is Mark.'

'Hey! Have those two got it together yet?'

'No idea. Guess we'll find out at the party.'

I'd had this bet with Chrissie that Mark and Zoë were bound to end up going out together. They were made for each other.

When I put down the phone I felt really lonesome. I missed Chrissie, she was my one and only good friend this side of the Atlantic. Maybe I'd make a big effort and get dressed and go round to the café instead of ordering something to be sent up to the room.

I got dressed in jeans and a sweatshirt and I was just making my way out through Reception when I bumped into Ingrid.

'Hi,' she said.

'Hello.'

'Where are you going?'

'Just to the café down the street for a bite to eat.'

'Maybe I'll join you,' she said.

56

I was so amazed I couldn't think of an excuse as to why not.

'Sure, go ahead,' I said.

So we walked to the café together in silence. Ingrid chose a table right by the window where everyone could see her. Sasha came over as soon as he caught sight of me and was really friendly.

Ingrid ordered a salad with smoked duck and a bottle of mineral water without so much as looking at him. It was pretty embarrassing.

I had what had become my favourite. A croque-monsieur, which is a rather grand-sounding name for a toasted cheese and ham sandwich. I always have loads of French mustard on mine. While we ate, Sasha stayed by the table to chat to us.

As he left, Ingrid leaned over and said to me, 'Do you want a bit of advice?'

I shrugged.

'Don't be too friendly,' she continued. 'People can take advantage, you know. Being with a model opens doors.'

I felt myself flush with anger. 'I don't know what you mean. He's a really nice person and a friend of mine, as a matter of fact.'

Ingrid looked at him with narrowed eyes. 'I guess he's OK – good-looking, in a way. But you'd be best to stick to your own crowd. It's important who you're seen with. Still, it's up to you. Don't say I didn't warn you.'

I was prickling all over with indignation, but I wasn't going to give her the satisfaction of seeing me admit to it.

'So tell me what sort of day you've had?' I asked, changing the subject with determination.

Ingrid went into a great spiel about the brilliance of her day. She'd been having fittings at Klavin's studio and, according to her account, a long list of minor celebs had dropped by just for the treat of seeing her there.

'How about you?' she ended.

I tried to see if I could break through her Nordic gloom by giving her a graphic account of me acting the reluctant ice-lolly, a zillion metres off the ground. But Ingrid was just about the most humourless person I'd ever come across. She just chewed her way through her salad as if I was giving a highly detailed narration of a trip to the dentist's.

When she'd finished eating, she did one of her disappearing acts.

Sasha came over.

'Your friend is very beautiful, but perhaps not so friendly,' he said.

'She's not really my friend,' I apologised. 'She's not in a very good mood, I'm afraid.'

'I see,' he said. 'Is she British? She seems so cold and reserved.'

'No – Swedish. Maybe it's the effect of all those icy fjords and long dark winters.'

He agreed. 'That must be it.'

Then he leaned forward and pretended to wipe the table. 'I can't stay long,' he said. 'The patron is here.'

He jerked a look over his shoulder.

I followed his gaze to a sour-looking man pacing up and down in front of the kitchens with his hands clasped behind his back.

'I have to work tonight,' Sasha continued. 'But tomorrow, maybe we could meet after four?'

I hesitated. Perhaps Ingrid was right and he was taking advantage of me.

'But of course you may have something better to do . . .'

Forget Ingrid, I thought.

'Of course not. I'll be here tomorrow outside at four.'

At that point Sasha straightened up and gave me a warning look.

The patron frowned in our direction and disappeared behind the bar.

'What's the problem?'

'If he catches me chatting to customers, I'll be fired. See you at four . . .' he said and hurried off, collecting empty glasses on his way.

Ingrid was ages as usual. When she returned to the table, she asked me: 'Are you going to the party at Les Bains tonight?'

'What party?'

'Haven't you been invited? It's this really smart nightclub.'

I shook my head.

'All the Tops are going, I'm surprised no-one's asked you.'

'I'm not one of the "Tops", Ingrid, in case you hadn't noticed. And besides, I have to be up at dawn, I've got a long day's shoot tomorrow. In fact, I think I might be making a move right now. I've got things to sort out.'

I took enough money out of my purse to leave Sasha a generous tip and left Ingrid to pay.

I could see Sasha's eyes following me as I made my way past the facade of the café and along the sidewalk. I gave him a little wave and a wink and he grinned back. He had absolutely *gorgeous* white teeth.

I spent the rest of the evening virtuously giving my hair a treatment and my skin a face-pack, and then got into bed early.

There was nothing on TV, so I went to sleep feeling a bit of a loser, actually. Ingrid was out having a night on the town and I was lying there like some middle-aged frump with face cream on and my hair all done up in jumbo rollers. Still, I guess that's what a model's life is all about. So much for the style and the glamour!

Six

From that moment on, things hotted up. Each day started with a wake-up call at some unearthly hour like 4.30 am, and then by 5.00 am the hair stylist and make-up artist would arrive. I soon discovered why I'd been given a suite. Most of the shooting was in central Paris so my pad became the head-quarters for a whole army of people whose lives seemed to be dedicated to making everything 'Klavin' exude sheer perfection. There was one girl who never said a word, but spent all day ironing, brushing and steaming, and practically going over garments with a magnifying glass in search of fluff.

I had been booked for five days to shoot the real-life sequences. In these I was meant to be rich, single and stylish – the ultra-perfect young Klavin woman going about her daily life. For each sequence I wore a different outfit: head-to-toe, totally outrageous, Klaus Klavin.

Most of the fittings had taken place in London and then the clothes had been sent back to Paris for minor adjustments. That first morning, the stylist arrived in Reception with ten Klaus Klavin designer-dress boxes. It took two uniformed porters to deliver them to my room. I felt like a film star!

The stylist put on white cotton gloves to unpack the boxes. Each outfit emerged from its crunchy tissue paper and was hung in the closet. Every item came complete with its Klavin monogrammed velvet-padded hanger. When she had finished, I stood staring into the interior of the closet like a kid looking in a Christmas shop window. There must have been over $50,000 worth of clothes in there. Each outfit hung there with its matching shoes beneath it. Boy! If Cherie could see me now.

I'd never realised so much went on behind the scenes in making a commercial. Each day while I was being prepared by hair and make-up, a load of other people were also hard at work at the location. From way before dawn, out in the Paris streets, the film crew would be manning what looked like a wartime operation. Unsightly signs and wires had to be moved or camouflaged. Streets had to be cordoned off. Sometimes even the actual street itself was considered too dirty and had to be washed. For the first day's shoot, the real traffic was diverted from this really wide boulevard and a whole lot of new traffic was employed just for the filming.

I arrived on the scene to find Julio gesticulating madly at some guys who had been too slow at getting some signs moved. The make-up girl and I just had to sit in one of the film crew's vans and wait until it was sorted out.

And then, just as it looked as if we were about to start filming, down came the rain. Everyone sat around and waited some more. Most of the crew smoked and played cards. I was longing for a cigarette, actually, but I didn't dare smoke because of my lipstick. By 12 pm my stomach was rumbling and I was feeling weak with hunger. But, oh boy, just as we were about to break for lunch, the rain stopped and the sun came out.

It seemed that Julio wanted to get this sequence shot with sunlight on the wet street. So suddenly everyone leaped into life. Basically, all I had to do was walk across this street wearing this absolutely knockout Klavin outfit. It was the palest ice-blue cashmere with the miniest miniskirt, a top just short enough to show an inch or so of bare midriff and a kind of little cape for a jacket. It was worn with thigh-high pale ice-blue suede boots.

The idea was that I had to walk across the boulevard with all this traffic bearing down on me and I had to make out like I hadn't even noticed it was there. As I reach halfway, this guy, Maurice, who's kind of the other main part, has to wind his window down as if he's about to bawl me out – in typical-Parisian-driver fashion – when he suddenly smells the perfume. That's when they cut in the bit of me as the Blue Angel. Maurice has to look so knocked out he's rendered speechless – and by the time he's recovered himself, I'm on the other side of the road. The first three takes I was absolutely *convinced* I was going to get run over.

After the fourth take, Julio Iononi stopped the shooting and hurried over to me.

'Ashe, what is with you, eh? You look like a leetle frightened animal. I want you 'ave big steps to cross

63

the road. Like this!' He did a hilarious demonstration. 'How you say . . . ?'

'Striding?'

'Striding, yes. Head up. Confident. Remember the statue. Victoire, eh? Not defeat.'

'Yes, sure, I'm sorry. It's just that – are you sure all these guys are going to stop?'

'All these drivers are very smart, very skilled. They're racing drivers . . .'

'That's what I thought.' His statement was hardly calculated to give me confidence.

'If they come as near as six millimetres, I will personally shoot them with my own hands,' said Julio.

'OK, OK. I believe you. I'll try again.'

'Wait!' said Julio and he called over a stylist. He pointed out the tiniest bit of a smudge on my boot. She brought a suede brush and brushed it off. That's perfectionism for you.

Anyway, by 3.30 pm, when we had done precisely twelve takes and I was practically dead from starvation, the clouds mounted up and it started to drizzle. Julio announced that we could call it a day.

Three-thirty. With any luck I could get back to the café before Sasha's shift ended.

'Am I needed any more?' Julio shook his head.

'Nothing more until tomorrow morning, 6.00 am. OK?'

I flagged down a cab and directed the driver to the café. I knew I really should go back to the hotel and change first. But I was starving and I didn't want to miss Sasha either.

Sasha was standing at the window looking out when I arrived. He opened the door for me and I swept through.

'Hey! I'm about to drop dead from hunger. Bring me food! Say, what do you think of the outfit?' I asked all in one breath.

'It's very nice.'

'Is that all you have to say?' He was being really off with me. 'It's Klaus Klavin.'

'It is very nice but it is not right for you.'

'Not right for me?'

'In France, young girls do not dress so . . .' he paused.

'So, what?'

'So obviously . . .'

I was furious. That was just so rude. What did he know about fashion anyway. How dare he!

'Well, thank you for your opinion. As a matter of fact I've come straight from the shoot. I didn't have time to get changed or I would have missed you.'

He shrugged his shoulders, still looking sullen.

'Come to think of it, I've changed my mind about eating, actually,' I said and stormed out.

Back at the hotel I had a shower and scrubbed all the make-up off my face. I stared at my reflection in the mirror. That's when I suddenly realised what he meant. French girls my age had this really natural look. It was a kind of understated chic, clean washed faces, simple hair styles, well-cut casual clothes, flat shoes. They didn't go in for all this dressy stuff like English and American girls did. I suddenly realised that by French standards I must have looked really tarty.

I pulled on a bathrobe and wandered thoughtfully out of the bathroom. I was just about to order something to eat from room service when there was a knock on my door.

'Pour vous, Mademoiselle.' A hotel porter stood outside with a large paper package.

I took it in.

Inside, wrapped in a napkin and still hot, was my favourite croque-monsieur with loads of mustard.

There was a note with it.

'I think I have said something very rude to you. Forgive me. I am waiting outside. Maybe you will want to speak to me again when you are not so hungry? Yes? Sasha.'

I ate the croque-monsieur and felt a lot better. Then I put on a pair of jeans and a T-shirt and made my way downstairs. Well, I didn't have anything better to do, did I?

Sasha was leaning against a lamppost with his back to me, smoking a cigarette.

'Hi.'

'I didn't think you'd come,' he said.

'It was the croque-monsieur that talked me round. Thanks.'

'Come on, then,' said Sasha. 'Let's get away from here. If I see that café for another minute I shall go mad.'

We walked towards the Metro.

'Am I dressed OK now? Do you approve? Like a good French girl and not like a big bad American?'

66

'It wasn't just the clothes.'

'What then?'

'Well, imagine how I feel, standing looking like, how you say – a pingouin . . .'

'A penguin?'

'Yes, a penguin. And you come in dressed like some millionaire's leetle darling.'

'But I'd come straight from the shoot. I told you that.'

We walked along in silence for a little longer. Then he stopped and threw his cigarette into a puddle and stood glaring at it.

'There's something else isn't there?' I prompted.

He shrugged and started walking again, faster this time. 'It's nothing to do with me,' he muttered.

'What isn't?' I was practically running to catch up with him, and it had started raining again.

'It was what your "friend" Ingrid said . . . Yesterday, after you'd gone.' He swung round to face me.

'Oh ye-es.'

'But I didn't believe her. It was just when you were dressed like that . . .' He started walking again.

'So what, precisely, did Ingrid say?' I was running after him, dodging huge raindrops. It was really starting to rain hard.

He stopped, turned to me and looked me in the eyes.

'That you got the job with Iononi instead of her because you were *nicer* to him.'

'Nicer to him?' There was rain running down my face now but I took no notice. 'You mean as in "*nicer*".'

'Yes.'

'But that's disgusting! He's middle-aged. He's practically bald, for heaven's sake! He's old enough to be my father!'

By this time we were standing in the middle of the road, ignoring the pouring rain. Cars were swerving and hooting at us.

'He's very famous. He goes out with lots of young girls, doesn't he?' said Sasha.

'Not this one, he doesn't. This one is *very* picky,' I said with determination.

I could tell by the expression on his face that Sasha believed me.

'Not too picky to go out with me this afternoon?' he asked, smiling for the first time.

'I'm not *going out* with you. I've only come to improve my French,' I said.

'Of course. This is strictly a business deal!' he said, holding up a battered camera case.

'But it's raining. You can't take pictures of me like this . . .' My face was dripping with rain and my hair was clinging to my head in rat's tails. The rain was coming down in torrents.

'But you look wonderful. That's exactly what I want. Here, take this . . .' Sasha took off his old mac and put it round my shoulders.

'You want to take pictures of me in the rain?'

Without responding, he knelt down and started clicking the shutter.

It was the Paris rush hour and the sidewalks were crowded with people heading for the Metro Station; people kept tripping over him. But he didn't care, he just went on taking pictures. Before I could stop him he was walking backwards down the sidewalk and out across the road.

'You're nuts! Totally insane!' I shouted, hurrying after him.

I forced my way against the current of people making their way through the downpour, heads bent, holding umbrellas up against the torrential rain. He dodged across roads, narrowly missing cyclists. In the effort to keep up with him, I got splashed head to foot by a passing truck. 'Great!'

At last, he stopped at a deserted café. It was a sad little place and it wasn't helped by the weather. Everything was saturated – its tables shone with pools of water. Sasha swept the water from a chair. 'Please sit down, just for a moment.'

'What! Here?'

'Don't smile,' he warned. 'Look straight at me.'

Frankly, I didn't feel like smiling. I was drenched to the skin. But he was drenched, too. His shirt was sticking to his body and, I couldn't help noticing, it was a very nice body.

'Perfect!' he announced. 'I have finished my film. Would you like a hot chocolate?'

'Do you think we could go *inside*?'

He held the door open for me.

'You are totally crazy. You know that, don't you?'

'Wait till you see the pictures.'

'But I must look some fright!'

'Do you know that famous old photographer – Robert Doisneau? That is what the pictures will be like. You'll see.'

'Never heard of him. What does he specialise in

– 'underwater'?' I shook the rain off his mac. It was saturated.

Sasha shook his head. 'Ordinary people just living their lives. Just simply shot in black and white. But brilliant . . .' He was winding the film back as he talked. It was a really old camera with a hand-crank.

'And you think that you can get decent pictures with that?' His camera looked like a museum exhibit.

'It belonged to my uncle. It's German – made before the war. It takes the most "superbe" pictures.'

'I'll believe it when I see it.'

'And now for your part of the deal.'

'My French lesson? Not sure if I'm up to it after all that.'

But Sasha wasn't going to take no for an answer.

You know, during the next half-hour, I realised what a curious language French is, like they have two ways of saying 'you' for starters. And there's a whole etiquette thing about when you can switch from calling people one to the other – like from 'vous' to 'tu'. And it's really over-the-top and gushy when you want to express any kind of emotion – like you can't just be happy to see someone – you have to be 'ravie' – and you're not just sorry you missed them – you're 'desolé' – like absolutely 'desolate'. But when it comes to actually saying something important like you 'love' someone, they go all cold and stand-offish and you can't be sure whether 'je t'aime' means 'I like you' or 'I love you'. Isn't that typically foreign and infuriating?

'So how can you tell the difference?' I asked.

He stared into his chocolate and then looked me straight in the eyes. 'How can you tell, anyway?'

'I guess I don't know.'

There was a kind of awkward silence after that.

Anyway, Sasha changed the subject and started telling me in slow French about the people who came into his café.

'And what about me?'

'You?'

'What did you think when I came into your café?'

'No, I can't tell you that.'

'Why not?'

'When you came in I was just too . . .' He paused. 'Bouleversé.'

'What does that mean?'

'Homework. Look it up,' he said.

Seven

When I collected my key from Reception there was a message for me from Lou-Lou, my London booker, to call her urgently, no matter what time.

I went up to my room wondering what could be up. I'd made my obligatory daily call into the agency before I'd gone out that afternoon. Something must have cropped up since. Maybe she had a casting for some important job lined up.

When I got through she said: 'Have you heard about the scandal?'

'No, what scandal? I've been out since I last called you.'

'Lisa Martinez has been suspended by Visage.'

Visage was the Paris agency I was subcontracted through. Lisa Martinez was one of their biggest names. She was skinny as a reed with cheekbones reaching to her ears practically and vast gorgeous eyes. She was known as 'Top-Cat' because she was Queen of the catwalk, and she'd just done this big underwear advertorial for one of the glossies – five whole pages featuring her alone.

'No, I don't believe it! Why?'

'There's been this big hoo-ha about that underwear feature she did last month. One of the magazine's really important advertisers, spending mega-bucks, has pulled out of this year's campaign with them. They've complained that she's too thin. Their theory is that ultra-thin models like Lisa are influencing girls into becoming anorexic.'

'I wouldn't be surprised if she *was* anorexic, she's really pale and kind of washed-out.'

'They've suspended her until she's put on five kilos.'

'Five kilos! That's rich!'

'So Visage are starting a big witch-hunt, checking out their girls. Any hint of an eating disorder and it's instant suspension.'

'Oh boy!'

'I thought I ought to warn you. You are eating OK, aren't you?' Lou-Lou sounded anxious. 'You're not exactly hefty yourself.'

'Of course! Making a real pig of myself.'

'So what have you had today?' asked Lou-Lou seriously.

I suddenly realised that I'd totally forgotten to eat. I'd had that croque-monsieur, but basically apart from that I hadn't given food a thought. I'd been too wrapped up in Sasha.

'OK, OK. I admit today has not been an ideal day. But tomorrow, back on the muesli and salads and tons of fruit. Does that make you happy?'

'The important thing is to eat properly. Once you get on those starve and binge trips, that's when the real trouble starts.'

'Three healthy meals a day, I promise!'

'That's the idea. And keep an eye on the other girls. It can be a real problem in this line of business.'

Before I went to bed I took out my little French–English dictionary. I flicked through the 'B's' until I got to 'bouleversé' – 'upset, overthrown, thrown into confusion', it said.

I smiled to myself – 'thrown into confusion' – like 'knocked out' maybe? I went to sleep feeling really happy. OK, I admit it, I was pretty knocked out by Sasha too.

Next morning I tucked into a big breakfast of muesli and fruit, and I even had scrambled egg, for goodness sake. Imagine being fired for being too thin! Boy, it wasn't going to happen to *me*.

Françoise, the make-up girl, was halfway through my make-up when the phone rang. She lifted the receiver with an impatient sigh. She hated being disturbed when she was working.

'It's someone called Sasha. Is it important?'

I nodded violently and she handed me the receiver.

'Hi! It's me. How are you?'

'I just wanted to know if you slept all right.'

That was just so adorable!

'Like a dream. How about you?'

'I did not sleep at all. I went for a long walk instead. I felt too good to sleep.'

I felt warm all over. Hey, this guy was losing sleep over me!

Françoise was signalling violently that she wanted to do my lip-line.

'When can I see you again?' he was asking.

'Look, I don't know. Honestly, I'll have to grab any moment I can. I'll come to the café, OK?'

'When?'

'I can't tell. Depends how long the shoot goes on. First minute I can get away.'

I put the receiver down.

'Is that your boyfriend?' asked Françoise with a frown as she made me make 'apple' cheeks for the blusher brush.

'Maybe,' I said. 'Yeah, well, yes. Why not?'

The warm feeling lasted all through that day. The shoot went like a breeze, as a matter of face. I had to do this sequence wearing Klavin sportswear, where I had to jog through this park with a massive dog wearing a Klavin monogrammed crop top and jogging pants – I mean me, not the dog. The dog had his own little monogrammed leather Klaus Klavin collar. And you know what? Everything was Klavin sapphire-blue – even the dog! It was this massive Borzoi – you know the kind with all that long shaggy fur? The dog looked absolutely unreal all blue like that – cool, eh? And it wasn't cruel or anything, 'cos I checked. I'm really careful about animals, I don't even buy make-up that's been tested on animals and that sure restricts you. The dog was dyed with stuff that would just wash out – so everyone was praying hard it wouldn't rain.

Anyway, I don't know who enjoyed the shoot more, the dog or me. He obviously thought jogging back-wards and forwards along this path through the Bois de Boulogne, was about the best thing that ever happened to him. Demon, that was the dog's name, and I had to jog past all these really hunky guys who were jogging in the opposite direction. And when I passed Maurice, who was the very last of the hunky guys – and he got a whiff of my perfume – you've got it, that's when they were going to cut in some of the Blue Angel footage.

All the time we were shooting, the camera was tracking backwards up the road in this van and the cameraman was kind of hanging out on a strap to get a really low angle. He got his face washed three times by Demon. It was a pretty hilarious morning.

I was just getting my breath back from Take Number, like, *sixteen* or something, when Julio's PA signalled to me. There was a call for me on her mobile.

It was Lou-Lou calling.

'Hey, guess what. Someone from Klaus Klavin's studio's been on the phone. Klaus flew in from New York this morning. He saw the rushes of the first day's shoot and now he wants to see *you*.'

'But he's seen me, hasn't he? On film? What more does he want to see?' I didn't like the sound of this.

'He wants to see you *in person*, stupid. Soon as you're through today.'

'What for?'

'They won't say.'

'Where? Wait! What do I wear? Hey – maybe he's not happy with the filming so far.'

'I've no idea, Ashe. When Klavin asks to see someone you don't start interrogating them on "why". You just jump to it. Wear something simple and basic.

Smart and short to show off those legs and not too much make-up, OK?'

She gave me strict instructions to ring Visage the minute I got back to the hotel and they would send a car round for me.

I finished the shoot with a throbbing heart. Maybe he loathed the footage we'd taken. Maybe I was going to get accused of starving myself like Lisa, and get thrown out. Or maybe someone had sussed my actual age . . . Oh boy, that was a real possibility. My mind raced. Klaus Klavin had just come over from the States. I started to have some paranoid thoughts. He'd met someone who knew me or Mom . . . He must have . . . The more I thought about it, the more this idea got fixed in my mind. I'd really blown it this time.

Soon as I was back at the hotel, I called Visage, then leaped in the shower and washed my hair. They were sending a car round for me in half an hour. There was no time to drop in on Sasha. I phoned Room Service for a club sandwich on rye and ate it while I dried my hair. Then I selected the most classic outfit I had in my repertoire – a black A-line mini, a tight white T-shirt and a black fitted jacket. I added a pair of classic Gucci loafers and assessed the effect in the mirror. Oh boy! I looked about twelve years old! In desperation, I switched to a black skin-tight mini dress and stilettos and a dash of my favourite pillar-box red lipstick. To hell with what Lou-Lou said: she didn't know I had the problem of being a good two years younger than I was meant to be.

The car Visage sent was a big black limousine

with tinted windows. I felt like I was going to my own funeral in it as it slid silently through the Paris streets. The further we went, the further my heart sank. This could well be the end of my modelling career. Suddenly I could see it all. I would be sent back to New York in disgrace. Back to school and Mom and that slob Carl. Back to Logan and his pathetic possessiveness. It would mean leaving Paris and, although I wasn't really ready to admit it, the worst thing of all was that I'd be leaving Sasha. I could just imagine his face when I broke the news.

The car took me upwards through tiny winding streets flanked by really ancient houses. We were heading through the hilly bit they call Montmartre. There were all these steep old streets that lead to that white basilica thing – the Sacré Cœur. The limo came to a stop outside a tall old building with a load of trailing vines tumbling over its walls.

I pressed the intercom and the door clicked open. Hey, weird! Inside, you know what? The outside was just a facade – inside, everything had been stripped out and replaced by an ultra-modern steel and chrome interior. A girl dressed in jeans and Klavin T-shirt led me up some echoing industrial metal stairs to a long open room at the top of the house. It had massive studio windows all round – giving the most staggering views right across Paris.

The room itself, however, was a scene of utter chaos. It was like some sort of mad factory. There were whole walls pinned with fashion drawings, books of fabric swatches and buttons and buckles. Women were working at huge cutting tables littered with bits of calico cut into odd shapes. On a kind of island surrounded by a sea of multi-coloured scraps of fabric, a little old lady was sewing furiously at an ancient treadle machine. A boy was carting around dummies half-pinned into bits of clothing. Everywhere there seemed to be people hard at work: pressing, cutting, steaming or just sorting through racks and racks of garments which were in the process of being put together or taken apart. It was a scene of barely controlled panic.

In complete contrast to all this frantic activity, there were about six girls lounging around on some low white sofas in a corner. All of them blonde, all of them stunning, all of them obviously models. One of them was speaking animatedly in French into a mobile phone.

The girl who'd brought me upstairs signalled for me to sit down and wait.

At the sight of me the girls all started to talk at once in totally unintelligible French. I sat there feeling like a toad that had gatecrashed a party of frogs – a total outsider. I was the only one who wasn't dressed in an absolutely casual T-shirt and jeans. OK, I know – I'd done it again!

One by one, the girls were called through into a further room. They'd be in there about ten minutes, then they'd re-emerge, grab their little black designer knapsacks and do a lot of kissing on both cheeks – three kisses for the *really* favoured ones – and head off down the stairs.

When at last it was my turn, I put on a brave face. I'd had scenes like this with the Head at my High School. I'd just have to brave it out. I could handle it.

I recognised Klaus Klavin the minute I came into the room. He was dark and unshaven – a style statement in himself – and wearing amazing round designer glasses. He seemed to be in a frantic state, he was talking non-stop into a mobile phone and had sweat running down his face. The girl who'd brought me upstairs managed to interrupt and introduce me and reminded him that he'd seen me in the Ange Bleu rushes.

I waited breathlessly. If there was going to be trouble it was going to start right now . . . But instead, he got up and walked over and shook me by the hand.

'Would you *believe* the problems I'm having with buttons!' he exclaimed. 'Did you know that the whole world could run out of blue pearl buttons . . . like I've had the last in Paris?'

I shook my head. 'No, I guess not.'

I was amazed. I'd always imagined Klaus Klavin to be German or French maybe. But he was most obviously American and from the wrong side of Brooklyn by the sound of it.

'What are these oysters trying to *do* to me? It's like they're trying to sabotage my show!'

The girl made comforting noises about couriering some over from Hong Kong. This calmed him down a bit.

'The rushes were really something,' he said. Then he turned and asked the girl, 'You sure they're her? They sure don't look like her.'

'They're me all right.' I said. 'At least, I'm the one getting paid for it.'

'Guess that proves it, then. Can you walk?'

'Walk?' I asked stupidly.

'I'd like to see how you are on the runway.'

'Yes, I guess I can walk.' (Now, you know and I know, I'd never done catwalk, but I wasn't going to admit that to *him*.)

'OK, let's see you, then.' He gestured towards a white catwalk shape that had kinda been chalked out on the floor. I could see the footprints of the girls who had gone before me. God, how I wished I wasn't wearing stilettos.

Anyway, this is where my modern dance lessons came in. I took a deep breath, thrust my hips out and, giving what I thought was a pretty good imitation of a catwalk 'sashay', strode down the 'runway', as he called it. I paused, did a turn, another pause, a pose and came striding back.

Klaus Klavin nodded. 'Now let's try it without the shoes,' he said.

This was easier. He nodded again. 'Interesting,' he said and signalled to the girl who noted something down on her pad.

I looked from one to the other of them.

Maybe there wasn't going to be a confrontation after all.

Klaus Klavin was shaking me by the hand again and saying something about seeing me real soon. It seemed I wasn't going to be exposed for fraudulently posing as a seventeen-year-old. They had finished with me. I was free to go.

Eight

It was five by the time I got back to the hotel. I threw some jeans on and rushed round to the café. But Sasha was nowhere to be seen. The older barman who always came in to take over from his shift indicated that he'd left.

'Très très fatigué,' he said and put his hands up in a sleeping gesture and raised his eyes to heaven to show just how tired Sasha must have been.

'Oh, I see, merci,' I said. It didn't seem as though he'd left a message for me or anything, so there was nothing for it but to go back to the hotel.

I spent a pretty miserable evening. After flicking through all the channels on TV and finding there was nothing worth watching, I went to see a Richard Gere movie. But they'd dubbed it in French and I couldn't understand *one* word. After that I grabbed a hamburger in McDonald's. OK, I know this wasn't what you'd call a healthy diet but I kinda needed something that reminded me of home – comfort food? And then I had an early night. Hey, it's a wild and glamorous life being a model, isn't it?

The following day was a free day because Julio and

the crew were doing some aerial stuff that was needed for the Blue Angel sequences.

I took the opportunity to have a long lie-in.

But no such luck, by 10 am I was woken by my phone ringing.

'Hi,' I said sleepily.

'Ashe? I am calling you from Visage. It's Marielle.'

Marielle was the boss of Visage. A real Parisienne dragon of the first order. She literally *never* calls anyone. I had only ever spoken to her PA.

I was immediately wide awake. *Here comes trouble*, I thought.

'I thought you ought to be the first to know. Klaus Klavin wants to feature you in the finale of his Defilé.'

'Défilé?' I repeated sounding stupid.

'Défilé de Mode. His Autumn/Winter Prêt-à-Porter. You must know they start next week. Of course, it's short notice . . . but I imagine Marco won't want you to miss an opportunity like this . . .'

I swallowed. The Klavin Prêt-à-Porter was known as the high point of the Paris catwalk shows. 'Why me?'

Marielle paused. 'Well, it would have been Lisa, of course. She's always been Klaus's favourite but you've probably heard – she's having to rest for a while.'

Resting – that's what they call suspension!

'When do I start?'

'Lou-Lou will fix up all the details but I just thought I would personally give you a call. Congratulations, and – oh, yes . . . we are giving a little party for Klaus this evening. Of course, you will come.'

Quite obviously, this was an order not an invitation.

'Of course.'

'Jack will come for you at eight, he'll take care of you. And – hold on a minute . . .' I heard a male voice in the background. 'And Klaus says drop into the Boutique any time today, to choose something to wear, anything you like, as a gift from him. Ask for Elaine, she'll know what would be suitable. It'll be a big Press night.'

As she rang off, I settled back on the pillows and wondered whether I was about to wake up – this must all be a dream.

The phone rang again.

It was Lou-Lou.

'Hey! How's the flavour of the month?'

'I'm not sure. You must have heard. Is this for real?'

'Sure is. Seems that when Klaus saw the rushes, he had this big brain-wave for his finale. Instead of ending with the standard bridal gown, he's doing a version of the Ange Bleu robe and using the show to launch the perfume.'

'So *that's* why he wants me.'

'There's only one problem though. You know and I know you've never done catwalk. Klaus doesn't.'

'Didn't he ask?'

'He kind of assumed you had. Everyone did. You must have put on a pretty good act.'

'I've done a lot of dance.'

'That's a big help. But do you really think you're up to a Collection? Maybe we should get you some training.'

'Don't fuss, Lou-Lou, it'll be a breeze. You know, hips out – head back. It's only walking, for heaven's sake. I can handle it.'

'If you say so. How's the shoot going, anyway?'

'We've got at least one more day. Oh, and I'm invited to a lush party for Klavin tonight. Lots of the Press will be there.'

'Do you think you can handle all this, Ashe?' Lou-Lou sounded anxious.

'No problem. I'll love it.'

'OK . . . But remember, when it comes to the Press don't say too much to anyone. If they ask why Lisa's not around – say you don't know. Just be sure you are looking your best and smile like there's no tomorrow. Oh, and don't drink. OK?'

'I don't drink anyway.'

'Marielle says we may have to get someone to look after your PR. In the meantime, someone called Jack is going to help . . .' said Lou-Lou.

'Jack? That's great. He's cool.'

'You watch out for those Parisian men, OK?' warned Lou-Lou.

'I've got my eye on one already.'

Lou-Lou sighed. 'I worry about you sometimes, Ashe. You sure you can't get your mother to fly over to stay with you for a while? Visage would pay.'

'My mother! You must be joking. She'd go totally off the rails. I'm the sane one out of the two of us.'

After that, I did my best to calm Lou-Lou down and prove how well I was coping.

When she rang off, I got up and wandered over to the window and stared out. This couldn't be happening to me. Here I was in Paris, just about to star in a Designer Collection. I had to ring Cherie right now and tell her. She'd be so proud of me!

Her voice was all muzzy the other end of the line. I realised guiltily that I hadn't spoken to her for over a week.

'Cherie, Mom, it's me, Ashe.'

'Where are you ringing from?'

'The hotel, you know the Criston . . . in Paris.'

'Yeah, course, I remember.' She sounded annoyed.

'You all right, Mom?'

'You just woke me up, that's all.'

I suddenly realised that in New York it must be the middle of the night.

'Gee, I'm sorry. I just had to tell you. Klaus Klavin wants me to feature in his Prêt-à-Porter show. To do the finale.'

'Do you think we could talk about this in the morning? I've got one hell of a headache.'

'Are you OK, Mom?'

'No, Carl walked out on me this morning, if you must know.'

I bit my lip. I wasn't going to say I told you so. And it was tough to say I was sorry when I truly wasn't.

'You never liked him, did you?' She sounded as if she'd been crying.

'Not wildly.'

'Well, looks like you were right. He took the contents of my purse with him, too.'

'I'm sorry, Cherie.'

'I'll cope.'

'Course you will.' Then I had a sudden thought. 'You must need some money?'

'I don't want to take money off you, Honey.'

'Don't be silly. I'm going to be really loaded any minute now. I'll get Lou-Lou to forward you some, OK?'

When I rang off, I lay in bed thinking for a while about the weird relationship between Mom and me. Cherie really couldn't cope. She never had been able to. When she'd been really successful and everyone had loved her, she'd been on an all-time high. I remembered times when she'd come into my room when I was a little kid, all dressed up for a party or something, looking a million dollars, and she'd kind of radiated love and happiness and success. And then when things had started going downhill she'd tried harder and harder. She'd worked out and worked out – and she'd had every treatment on offer. There wasn't an inch of her body that hadn't been massaged and skin-peeled and bronzed and liposuctioned and de-cellulited. But whatever she'd tried, the magic had simply never come back. And she couldn't understand why not.

I wandered back to the window and stood there, staring blankly into space.

When younger and more stunning girls had taken Cherie's place, she'd clung to men like Carl who still treated her like a babe. It's as if she was clutching at the last remnants of her self-respect. And now even Carl had gone.

I shivered. One thing was for sure. Whatever happened, I wasn't going to end up like Cherie.

Nine

When I was a kid I used to have this one big fantasy – that Mr Bloomingdale had rung me up and invited me over to his store and I was going to be allowed to choose anything I liked – anything – for free. In this fantasy I'd go into the store and there'd be nobody there but me and Mr Bloomingdale and all these posey assistants who usually treat you like nobody. But because Mr Bloomingdale was there they'd be really really nice to me and helpful too while I hunted through the store trying and rejecting things. And I'd be in agony having to make the decision for just one item from all this incredibly classy Bloomingdale stuff. In the end, I'd settle for the naffest thing – like this pair of diamanté-encrusted sandals I'd seen in their window. Were they *gross*?

Well, that day, being given the freedom of Klavin's store to choose any outfit I liked for the party had exactly the same kind of feeling. It was as if that dream had become reality.

Firstly, I had to dress up to go there. I took a lot of care over this, right down to wearing my most expensive designer underwear. So, looking my best, right down to the bare skin, I strode into the showroom feeling like a million dollars on legs. My, was this living!

I was asked to take a seat on a big white silk love-seat while Elaine was summoned from the backroom.

Now, I imagined that choosing a Klavin outfit would just be a matter of a quick rake through the racks to see what they'd got. But, apart from a few transparent Klavin dummies hanging around wearing nothing but Klavin belts, there wasn't a shred of clothing in sight.

Elaine was expecting me. She was polished, crisp and efficient – a real showroom tigress. She asked what I 'had in mind'. I explained about the party. But she seemed to have all the details already and my measurements, too – she had been thoroughly briefed.

'How about I just show you a few things. And we'll take it from there.'

At a signal from Elaine, one by one, assistants came out carrying the most outrageous Klavin outfits. There was an off-the-shoulder dress cut on the diagonal in my most favourite pillar-box red. And there were some wickedly see-through numbers in a mixture of satin and floaty chiffon. And there was one made of three sections of shiny sapphire satin joined together by what looked like diamond-cut crystals. I had meant to choose something discreet and deadly sophisticated . . . But . . .

This was irresistible! It looked pretty spectacular off, but, when I tried it on, that couture cutting came into its own. It had a really tiny top joined to a mini skirt with two vast crystals, and at the back two thin straps crossed to join the waist at another crystal. Inside, it was totally lined with the softest silk. It felt like magic. I did a turn in front of the mirror. Elaine nodded her approval.

'I love it! I've just got to have this one.'

'Ah! But wait . . .' said Elaine, and she summoned a woman who had been standing by with a pin-cushion and a tape measure.

The dress felt perfect to me, but Elaine was not satisfied until the fitter had found some minute adjustments to make.

'But I need it for tonight,' I objected. 'It feels fine, really.'

'It will be at your hotel by 7.30 pm,' said Elaine. 'And it will be perfect.'

It seemed whatever I said I wasn't going to be allowed to take the dress away with me. So I contented myself with selecting a pair of strappy Klavin evening shoes to match.

I wandered down to the café carrying my Klavin carrier-bag so that all the world could see it and feeling très chic.

It was the lunch hour and the café was absolutely packed with people eating. I managed to find a table in a corner and catch Sasha's eye. He was serving the tables that were laid out for lunch. By the look of it he was being run off his feet. He was carrying at least three plates of food at a time, balanced precariously up his arm. He raised an eyebrow in the direction of the kitchens. The patron was standing by the swing doors watching every move he made like a sergeant major.

I ordered a Coca Lite from the other waiter and I saw Sasha stop him and hand something to him as he passed by. When my drink arrived, the little paper bill had scrawled on it: '*I must see you. Can we spend the evening together? S*'.

I turned the bill over and wrote: '*I'm busy tonight. But free till seven pm. A*'.

When I finished my Coke, I carefully laid out the money for it on the little plastic saucer and placed the folded bill in a prominent position.

I got up to leave, signalling with a look across to Sasha to pick it up. But, just my luck! Monsieur le Patron must have had second sight or something. He swept over to my table and picked up my empty glass, together with the incriminating bill.

Then he opened the door for me and, with a little half-bow of the head, said: 'Mademoiselle, bonne journée.'

Bonne journée to you too, you creep, I fumed to myself. *Now* what was going to happen? I made my way back to my room, really worried.

I didn't have to wonder long.

Within half an hour, the girl on Reception rang up to say there was someone waiting for me downstairs.

I emerged from the lift to find Sasha standing in the lobby with a crushed carrier-bag that looked as if it had all his possessions in it. He had a totally pissed-off expression on his face.

'They haven't fired you?'

'Yes, they have. I should have been more careful.'

'But it was my fault. I feel terrible. Maybe I could go and persuade them to take you back?'

Sasha shook his head. 'It's not the first time. I'm always in trouble. It was a boring job anyway. Come on, let's go. I want to get away as fast as I can from that leetle Hitler – le Patron.'

'Where shall we go? I've only got two hours or so.'

We were out on the street and Sasha was lighting a cigarette.

'I don't know. Anywhere . . .' he said dragging on it with determination.

And then he gave me a mock evil grin.

'I know where we'll go. Somewhere to match my black mood,' he suggested.

'You mean like a horror movie or something?'

'Wait and see,' he said and started walking at a fast pace. 'If we want to get there in time we have to hurry.' He took my hand and practically ran with me down into the Metro Station.

We had to change a couple of times on the Metro and then we eventually emerged at a station called Denfert-Rochereau.

'Denfert or d'enfer. That means "of hell",' said Sasha. And he started to make faces like a devil as he led me towards an entrance that said '*Entrée des Catacombes*'.

'Catacombs – isn't that where they put dead people?' I asked.

'Yes, it is!' he said and pulled me forward by the hand. 'This is the place I come to when I feel really bad.'

He paid for two tickets at a 'guichet' and then led the way down a long eerie flight of stone steps that seemed to go on forever. When at last we reached the bottom, the ceiling dripped on my head and it was squelchy underfoot. In the dim light it was as much as I could do to keep up with Sasha's shadowy body as he led the way through a maze of narrow dark passages. And then, as my eyes grew accustomed to the gloom, I noticed there were piles of bones stacked up on either side of us, built into the walls. As we rounded a corner, we were confronted by a great pile of skulls.

'Are these bones real *human* bones?' I asked with a shiver.

'Of course,' he said. 'They're from the big plague of two hundred years ago.'

'That's really gross,' I said and shivered again. I mean, back home, things like that aren't left around. When people die it's all kind of hushed up like it hasn't really happened, with loads of flowers and music and stuff. I couldn't believe it – these Europeans with all their bones and relics were so damn primitive.

'It's not gross. They're just bones.'

'I really don't like this,' I said. It suddenly felt claustrophobic and cold and clammy. 'Why did you bring me here?'

'Look, Ashe. It's OK, we'll leave,' said Sasha. He put his arm around me. 'Look, these are just dry old bones. Two hundred years old. It's nothing! Some people I know even used to have parties down here.'

'Parties! Now that is *really* morbid and disgusting.'

I shivered again and Sasha held me a little closer.

His body was warm against mine and, in spite of our current location, I felt good about being so close to him. I'd never felt like this with Logan. I know I'd been meant to and always thought it was my fault that I hadn't. But this was different.

As we stumbled back into the sunlight I was kind of laughing with relief at being out of that place and shaking at the same time. Sasha led me to a little traffic island in the middle of the street where there were some trees and a couple of benches.

'Oh, that's better. Sunlight! Fresh air!' I gasped.

Sasha pulled me round to face him. I guess I must still have been looking pretty shaken because he said:

'I'm sorry. You didn't enjoy that at all, did you? And I thought you were such a strong, hard American woman.'

And then, quite suddenly, he had his arms around me and we were kissing right there in broad daylight in the middle of the square. A passing motorist tooted his horn and shouted: 'Bravo. Allez-y.'

And then we were both laughing and we sat down on one of the benches and he kissed me again in a more kind of slow and meaningful way. And then Sasha brushed my hair back from my face and said:

'You know, there is one thing that really worries me about you.'

'What's that?'

'I think you must have a great big cowboy boyfriend back home.'

'And I guess you have a really petite and sexy

French girlfriend, called Nicole or something.'

'I did. But not called Nicole. And not any more.'

'Same here. Not any more.'

'So he won't want to come and punch me on the nose?'

I shook my head. 'Just let him try,' I said. 'What about your girlfriend? Will she come and haunt me like in *Fatal Attraction*?'

'You don't own a rabbit, do you?'

I shook my head.

'That's a good thing.'

After that we just started talking. It was like we had so much to say to each other. I can't remember exactly what. I guess we talked about Logan and Sasha's ex-girlfriend and our families and stuff. We decided to walk some of the way back. But every time we came to a Metro Station we decided against going down into it and taking the train and walked some more. We just walked and talked and talked and walked. I can't remember ever being able to talk to anyone like that before. And then, almost before we knew it, we found we'd walked all the way back to the Criston.

'Hey, what's the time?' I asked.

'Seven-thirty,' said Sasha.

'It *can't* be. I'm going to be late. I've got to fly!' I said.

'But when will I see you again?'

'I don't know! Come to the hotel. Leave a message. I am going to get *killed*! I'll be fired too, if I don't hurry.'

I left Sasha standing on the sidewalk looking lost and holding his crumpled carrier-bag.

I felt pretty bad about it, if you want to know.

Ten

The Klaus Klavin party was being held in this lavish apartment on this really classy street called the Avenue Foch.

The apartment was in a house that was totally over-the-top gorgeous. You went in through these massive doors, and inside was a courtyard with a garden. The house was built like a palace, all stone and covered in scrolls and curlicues and jutting-out bits carved like garlands of fruit and leaves. Inside, a massive curving fairytale stone staircase led upwards. It was flanked by big iron lamp-holders with real flames burning in them. At the top was a set of rooms that was absolutely packed with the most posey-looking people I'd ever set eyes on.

I was glad I had Jack with me. Jack seemed to know exactly what to do. He just placed one hand on the small of my back and paraded me round as if I was the biggest thing that had hit Paris since the Revolution.

'You must meet Ashe,' he kept saying. 'She's Klavin's big new discovery.'

Before long people were calling to me: 'Ashe' – 'Ashley', and camera flashes kept dazzling my eyes.

Jack was directing me as to when to smile and telling me 'who-to' and 'who-not-to' talk to and following up each introduction with killing bits of gossip about the people we met. He seemed to know simply everyone.

'Am I glad you're here,' I whispered to him.

'And I'm glad you're here, Ashe. I haven't had so much fun in ages. For once everyone is taking notice of me. Hey, come on, let's say "hi" to Klaus.'

Someone tapped me on the shoulder at that point and a voice said: 'Mind if I join you?'

I looked round. It was Ingrid. She kissed me on both cheeks like a long-lost sister – she was being really friendly for some reason.

'Love the dress,' she said eyeing it through assessing eyes. 'It's Klavin, isn't it?'

'Umm, isn't it just heavenly? I've got to thank him for it.'

'He gave it to you? You *must* be popular.' She gave me a meaningful look. You know, Ingrid was one of those people who have a knack of turning everything you say around and making it sound bad.

'Only for the publicity,' I said, before she could get any ideas.

'Oh, sure,' agreed Ingrid in the most unconvinced tone. 'What size is it?' she asked abruptly.

You know, Ingrid was *weird* at times. 'An eight, I think, why?'

'That's what I thought,' she said.

This interrogation was interrupted by Klaus Klavin. He was surrounded by a dense crowd of admirers, but he broke free and came straight over when he caught sight of us. He put one arm round me and the other arm round Ingrid and called over a photographer who took a load of pictures of the three of us. Ingrid seemed to cheer up a lot after that and became quite animated for her.

As the evening progressed, the voices got louder and louder, and the room became more and more crowded. Actually, as I looked around I realised practically everyone was middle-aged. It was getting pretty boring being paraded around with a fixed grin. So boring, in fact, that in spite of my better judgement, I had actually drunk a glass or two of champagne. I guess I wasn't used to it. I was starting to feel rather hot and hazy.

'How long do I have to stay here?' I whispered to Jack. 'This is getting to be a real drag.'

'You want to go somewhere more exciting?'

'Isn't Paris night-life meant to be the best in the world?' I guess the champagne was really getting to me.

'OK,' said Jack. 'Let's go. You've made your appearance. We'll take you somewhere much more fun.'

'We?'

'Me and Maurice. He's waiting downstairs.'

Now Maurice and I had never really hit it off. One major problem was that he did not speak one word of English. And you know what my French is like. So communication between us was basically a joke.

If ever you want a guided tour of Paris night-life, you couldn't do better than hire Maurice and Jack. They knew everywhere – and every*one* knew them.

The art, it seemed, was to breeze into a place, stay just long enough to get noticed, and then move on.

We started at a bar called The Barfly which was absolutely packed with what Jack called 'BCBG' (Bon Chic Bon Goût) – the rich and stylish Parisians who were the most arrogant of all. Then we went on to the club Ingrid had mentioned called Les Bains, so called, apparently, because it's in a building which used to house the old Turkish baths. Jack pointed out the words '*Bains Douches*', still written up outside.

Les Bains had what they called a 'Nuit Mannequin' and the place was so jam-packed with stunning girls you could hardly slip a credit card between them.

'Jolies meufs,' Maurice commented to Jack.

'What's a meuf?'

'You, my darling, are a "jolie meuf". It's the latest Parisian slang. Everything backwards. "meuf" equals "femme". A bloke is a "mec" from "ce monsieur" – "ce M." – backwards.'

After that Jack and I set to work confusing Maurice by making up ridiculous backwards American slang. We took a 'bac' to the next 'bulc' which was called the 'Casbah' or rather the 'Habsac'. Inside we bumped into a load of photographers from the party who insisted on taking more pictures of me and Jack and Maurice. Maurice was a bit the worse for wear by this time and Jack and I were kind of supporting him.

We ended up somewhere called the Marrakesh. By this time I had managed to persuade Jack that there was no point in going to bed, as Maurice and

I had to be up for a dawn start anyway. It was about three in the morning and the crowds were thinning somewhat. So much so we even found a corner to sit down in.

Maurice instantly fell asleep. He kept kind of slumping and practically squashing me until Jack propped him up again. I was killing myself with laughter, it was just such a mad crazy evening.

Jack became quite quiet at that point and I sat watching a young couple slow-dancing. I suddenly felt really lonely and wished that Sasha could be there.

'It's really good of you to take me out like this,' I said.

'I haven't had such a great time in ages,' said Jack.

'But haven't you got someone special, like a girlfriend or something, you'd rather be with?'

'Un petit ami?' asked Jack.

I nodded.

'He's asleep on your shoulder.'

'Maurice!'

'Don't sound so surprised. He's not that ugly.'

'I just hadn't realised . . .' I said.

You know, sometimes I reckon I go around with my eyes closed, I'm so caught up in my own little world.

By the time we got back to the Criston it was 4.15 in the morning. I know I should have been getting my beauty sleep, but a girl has to live a little sometimes!

I arrived at my door to find Françoise banging on it like she was trying to break it down. She looked like thunder. I realised guiltily that my make-up call had been half an hour ago. She'd been knocking for ages, apparently.

This was the morning of the final shoot. The timing was absolutely crucial because we had to catch the dawn. If we didn't get the sequence we needed, we'd have to do the whole thing again the next day, and then the next, and so on, until it was right. And this would cost loads of money. So everyone was pretty tense.

I could hear Françoise grumbling to herself outside while I took a shower, so I called up Room Service and asked them to send up a really swanky breakfast for two with orange juice and champagne – that should sort her out. When I emerged from the bathroom the breakfast had arrived. Françoise thawed a little when I poured her a big glass of champagne and orange juice.

'Just to say I am 'très désolée', Françoise.' She even smiled as she had a sip. And then she took one look at the dark rings under my eyes and gave me a big lecture about getting enough sleep while she went to work with the concealer.

For this shoot I had to wear a Klavin evening dress. It was literally just a few drapes of palest ice-blue chiffon attached to a strapless top that was held on as if by magic. To be doubly sure it wouldn't slip, I had to be glued into it with a kind of rubbery carpet glue. And I had on the tiniest high-heeled strappy sandals. It was like a mini-mini-version of the Ange Bleu robe – but really minimal.

The sequence went like this. I had to walk across the Pont des Arts – which is this really old bridge over the Seine. I was meant to look as if I'd just left a party or something (which wasn't too difficult). Maurice is leaning over the bridge staring into the water, looking as if he's just left the party, too, and as I pass he turns. I morph into the Ange Bleu, and then morph back into the real-life girl and Maurice recognises that we've been one and the same girl all along. It all kinda ends in one big clinch. That's when the slogan comes up on the screen: *'Ange Bleu – woman or illusion?'*

Heaven knows how Jack had sobered Maurice up. But he was there on time and he was also, most surprisingly, able to stand up. We managed to get eight takes done before the sun had risen too high. And then Julio announced that we could call it a day.

Jack was waiting with a cab parked by the kerb.

'You checking I'm not getting too friendly with your petit ami?' I asked.

He shook his head. 'I'm here on a strictly pro-fessional basis. Marielle says I am to take you back to the hotel to change and then you are to go straightaway over to Klavin's studio,' he announced.

'But I haven't even slept yet!'

'And whose fault is that?' he said, waving a finger at me.

I think maybe Jack was feeling worse for wear from the night before. He waited while I changed at the hotel, then directed the driver to take me up to

Montmartre while he headed home to sleep, lucky thing.

The first person I set eyes on when I got to the studio was Ingrid.

'Hi,' she said. 'Join the queue.'

There were three other girls lounging on the sofa smoking. Ingrid seemed to know them all but she didn't introduce me.

They were going on about Jean Paul Gaultier, and Helmut Lang and a load of Prêt-à-Porter shows they had all been in together. One of the girls, Australian by the sound of it, was complaining in a whining voice to the girl beside her about flying all the way to Milan only to find that they'd over-booked models for the show and she wasn't needed. The girl she was talking to was smoking Gitanes. She nodded sympathetically and blew a perfect smoke ring: 'If I counted the times I'd been chucked out on my ear – people treat you like cattle unless you're a name – I'd have a breakdown if I didn't have a sense of humour. Still, you win some, you lose some . . .'

'It's OK if you can get a commercial,' continued the Australian girl. 'That kind of money can keep you going for a year or more.'

Ingrid said nothing and uncrossed and recrossed her legs, staring out of the window fixedly.

'How long have you been waiting?' I asked the Australian girl.

'Only an hour. I actually got to the point of getting fitted but then a couple of Tops arrived and I got shoved back again.'

'Know who's in there at the moment? . . . The Body. She just swept straight in. It's all about who you are, Baby . . .' said the girl with the Gitanes, blowing another ring. 'Here. You smoke? What's your name?'

'Ashe,' I said. But I declined the cigarette. I reckoned I'd done enough to wreck my health recently.

'*You* are Ashe Garnett?' she asked, looking at me as if she didn't believe me.

'That's right,' I said, wondering how she knew my surname. It was at that point that The Body swept out. Klaus Klavin's PA put her head round the door and caught sight of me.

'Ashe . . .' she said. 'So you made it. Can you come in right now?'

'Me? Umm, I'm pretty sure I'm not next,' I said.

'Oh yes you are. In here. Now,' she said. She evidently wasn't taking no for an answer.

I got up feeling really hot and embarrassed. I could hear a murmur of disapproval from the girls left on the sofa.

Klaus Klavin was in even more of a flap than the last time I'd seen him. His desk was a positive landslide of papers, drawings, pieces of calico and books of fabric swatches. He was smoking like crazy and attempting to balance a mobile phone under each ear as he waved sheets of fax paper at his PA.

'Do something about New York. *W* magazine are going to crucify me, I know it. And send Christy flowers. She's got a sore throat. And – Ashe, you are here – good! How did the shoot go? Don't tell me. If we go into another day we're way over budget.

Strip her down, Julie, and get her into the finale number.'

I was whisked behind a calico screen through which I could still hear Klaus droning down the phone – or rather phones.

'OK, put Mom through . . . Putting you on hold, Mom – your tickets arrived OK? Right, usual thing – Sam will be at Charles de Gaulle. No, don't bring me bagels, you can get them here. You're on hold now, OK? So . . . Manuel . . . Have the shoes arrived? Chase them – OK? Threaten. Tell them they're blacklisted. Do anything. OK, Mom, you're leaving for the airport? That's great, yes . . .'

By the time he had sorted his mother out, I was dressed in this amazing creation made of acres of flowing icy-green-blue-coloured chiffon crimped into the finest ripples. It had a veil, too, which was so light it rested over my head like a cloud – I could hardly feel it across my face. It was like walking in a breath of air. The fabric rippled with every movement I made.

Julie pulled back the screen.

'Yes . . .' said Klavin. 'Oh yes, yes, yes! Move . . . Turn . . . Beautiful . . . Ashe, I love you. You know that? I love you forever. When we have the shoes . . . Oh, yes. This is to be a show-stealer. Walk again. Turn . . . And as you turn just lift back the veil . . . Right. Ashley, you are *something*, you know that?'

'OK, so what else is she going to wear?' asked Julie.

'I don't know and I don't care. Put her in anything. I want her to do all the highlight numbers . . .'

Julie murmured something about 'experience'.

'She'll be fine. Won't you, Ashe? Specially in blue, anything blue for her skin tone.'

The fitting went on for over an hour. I couldn't help thinking guiltily of the other girls waiting outside. But there was nothing I could do about it. I was hauled in and out of an endless succession of garments until six had been selected and I was released.

Ingrid was let in after me. As she swept past she said under her breath: 'You took your time.'

I didn't retort. What could I say? It was hardly my fault.

Julie saw me into a cab, fussing like mad. 'Now, I want you to go and lie down. Promise me. Don't do a thing. Just take a bath and relax. And get something to eat. You look all in. See you at the Carrousel du Louvre at six-thirty. It's a vital rehearsal – music, technical and special effects. It'll be just you and a few of the other girls. Mainly for the technical bods. But your part is really important because that's the Ange Bleu launch.'

She must have caught sight of my face at that point because she added:

'You're going to be terrific. You know that, don't you?'

I nodded weakly. I was just about asleep already.

Back at the hotel, as I picked up my key, the receptionist passed over a message scribbled on a piece of hotel paper.

I came but you were not here. I will come by

again. I am walking all over Paris, looking for a job. But I am imagining you are with me, so I am not alone. Bisous, Sasha.

Eleven

The catwalk stretched away like a long icy mountain pass. I had never seen one so high or so narrow. It was made of what looked like crystal and the sides were modelled like ruggedly-cut rock.

'What's it made of?' I turned to Jack.

'Don't ask!' he said. 'Apparently it cost a small fortune. That's why Klavin's so uptight about the whole show. Full-scale rehearsals and everything. The Ange Bleu launch is the biggest thing he's done in years. He's literally gambling millions on it. He's based his whole Collection round it.'

His voice was interrupted by a burst of sound from behind the catwalk area.

'Rimsky-Korsakov,' said Jack.

'Who's he?' I asked.

'It's the music for the finale. It's called *Night on a Bare Mountain*.'

'That figures,' I said. 'That catwalk looks lethal. Like it's made out of ice or something.'

'I'm assured it's non-slip,' said Jack. 'Hey, this place looks great, doesn't it?'

The Klavin show was taking place in the galleries

underneath the Louvre. The whole area had been cordoned off from the public and was crawling with security guards. Jack had passes to take us through and soon we were standing in a tented area all done in the Klavin colours of gloss-black, gold, sapphire and beige. Jack led the way through the lush auditorium to backstage where we all had to change.

Backstage was in stark contrast to all the carpeting and glitz and flowers and stuff front of house. Here there was just a load of makeshift tables and stacking plastic chairs and racks and racks and racks of clothes. Two girls were already changing, stripped down to the barest underwear and totally unfazed at being in full view of everyone.

A little dumpy woman was going through a rack of clothes which had a piece of paper with my name Scotch-taped to it.

'That's me,' I said.

'Voilà,' said the woman: 'I am your dresser, Hortense.' She looked at a list in her overall pocket. 'I am just checking. I cannot find shoes for the finale. Do you know what they are like?'

'I know there was some fuss about them not having arrived yesterday.'

'Alors,' she said. 'It is always the same. One year a girl had to go on at the last minute with no shoes – the panic – tu ne peux pas imaginer!'

I cast an eye over the racks. There were just a few of the clothes I had tried on that morning in their sealed cellophane dress bags.

'Yes,' said Hortense following my gaze with pro-fessional disapproval. 'Only 'alf what I need is 'ere.

Always is everything changing – always nothing 'ere until at the last minute!'

'OK,' said Jack. 'Here's where I leave you. Going to have a few drinks with some Press guys and talk you up, Ashe.'

'You mean tell them how wonderful I am?'

'Something like that.'

'OK. Go for it.'

I was starting to get butterflies, actually. And my nerves weren't helped by the arrival of – yes, you've got it. Ingrid.

She strode into the room.

'Hi,' she said to me. 'Lucky for you we're having a rehearsal. This is your first show, isn't it?'

A couple of the other girls looked up and stared at me with interest.

'Speak up a bit, Ingrid. I don't think they heard you at the back,' I said.

Then she started going through the clothes on her rack and grumbling at her dresser about them being in the wrong order or something. One of the other girls came over to me. She was bronzed and stunning with slanting Slavic eyes.

'It isn't *really* your first show, is it?' she asked in an Eastern European accent – Russian, I think.

I nodded. 'I'm afraid so.'

'Everyone has first show or we would not be here – no? Do not worry. Is easy. Do everything as we do.'

A voice called out at this point: 'Mademoiselle Ashley Garnett, s'il vous plait.'

A motor-cycle messenger in a crash helmet with

111

his radio blaring came hurrying through the room carrying a big box.

'Ici voilà,' called Hortense. 'Enfin!'

Inside were the shoes for the finale. As she lifted them out my heart sank. They were made out of transparent Perspex, sculpted like rock. They had cross-over straps and underneath – you guessed it – massive platforms.

'Oh no, not platforms,' I said.

'Voilà, you see at the latest moment they 'ave arrived,' said Hortense taking them out with a glow of triumph on her face. 'Try them, please, for size.'

Actually, they weren't just platforms. They were more like stilts. Once balanced on them, I could barely walk.

Ingrid looked over at me and said helpfully:

'They're just like the ones Naomi was wearing when she fell over at the Vivienne Westwood show. Hard luck.'

For the rehearsal we didn't have make-up or anything, so it was just a matter of throwing clothes on and going through the moves. And I didn't have to wear the platforms until the finale, which was a relief.

I wasn't the first on, so I watched from the wings as each girl took her turn. There was a guy called Michel wearing earphones, who stood by and directed each of us on at the right moment. It was pretty straightforward – just a stride down the length of the catwalk, a stop to pose, then a U-turn and U-turn back, another pose and a straight walk back again. The only tricky part was when two girls had to pass each other on the narrow runway. It just meant you had to be aware of where the other girl was all the time and make sure that when you passed, you weren't swinging round or anything.

The Russian girl was coming off just as I went on. She winked at me. 'Good luck. Break a leg. Yes?' she said.

As luck would have it the music at this point was a number I had actually studied in my dance class – it was by another Russian composer, Prokofiev. It was really easy to walk to actually – it made you stride.

As I strode down the catwalk with the lights on me, I became aware of some figures in the audience, behind the sound engineers. I could just make out the silhouette of Klaus Klavin. He was studying my every move. But I didn't let this put me off; I just took a deep breath and gave him a confident smile as I stopped to pose.

The rehearsal was going really well until we reached the point where I had to wear the platforms.

I just gritted my teeth and took the walk at a slower pace, allowing three beats to every step instead of two. I was on my way back down the runway when I had to pass Ingrid.

I couldn't swear she did it on purpose, but as we came level with each other, she caught the edge of my platform against hers. I stumbled at this point and some hands were clapped and the music came to an abrupt stop.

I heard Klavin's voice, he sounded really tense and angry.

'Can we do that again from the top, please. From Ingrid's entrance – OK?'

My knees were shaking by this time and my ankle was starting to feel the strain. The next time we did it, it was even worse. I was so shaky, I turned too soon and nearly collided with Ingrid. The music came to a stop again.

Ingrid just stood in a slouched position on the catwalk as if I was the biggest lame-head that had ever lived.

'What seems to be the problem, girls?' asked Klaus.

'I can't work with amateurs, that's all,' said Ingrid.

I could feel my face burning. The other girls had come out of the backroom and were hovering at the entrance.

'And another thing. I'm not used to going on with a kid. Do you know how old she is?'

There was a deathly silence. I waited for the bombshell to break. Here it came. Why hadn't I come clean about my age from the start?

Klaus studied us both for a moment with his arms crossed: 'Frankly, Ingrid, I don't give a damn. I don't care if she's still in diapers. As long as she can toddle down that runway, she's doing the finale. OK? Maybe you're not happy doing this show, Ingrid. I think it might be best if Katya took over from you. OK?'

Ingrid stormed past me into the changing room.

'We'll do it again, from the top. And this time we'll get it right,' said Klaus quietly.

'So, how did the rehearsal go?' asked Jack as we

sat in the Café Marly an hour or so later.

I shook my head. 'Don't ask. I just hope it goes better tomorrow.'

'Know what they say about a bad dress rehearsal?' he said.

'Yeah, sure, but it's kind of like the first performance is the *only* performance. Doesn't leave much room for improvement, does it?'

'I heard some rumour about a clash of personalities?'

'Oh, me and Ingrid? I'm not telling tales outta school.'

'Good girl,' he said. 'Oh, and by the way, my friends in the media have been hard at work. I've got some cuttings of last night's coverage. Take a look. It's looking pretty good.'

He took out a fluttering pile of press cuttings from his brief-case. As he flattened them out on the table I could see that there were several pages with pictures in which I featured. There was one with a headline from *Le Figaro*.

'What does that mean?' I asked Jack.

' "Has Klavin found a new muse?" Nice one, eh? And there's a pretty good picture of you underneath. Klaus is over the moon. Just what he needs to get them panting for the launch tomorrow. People are already selling their souls for invitations.'

I looked through the pile. There were a whole lot of posey pictures with me shoulder to shoulder with a load of minor celebs at that classy party in the Avenue Foch. And then there were even more of me and Jack and Maurice, taken when I was barely aware of the photographers, on our rave night out on the town. There was one with Jack on one side and Maurice leaning over me dead drunk. It looked like he was positively drooling over me – biting my neck or something. It had the headline: '*L'amour hors du tournage?*'

'Hey, that one's a bit out of line! Even I can translate that word. "L'amour" – that's "love"! They trying to imply Maurice and I have something going?'

'Oh, come on, it's got a question mark after it, hasn't it?'

'But that's not on.'

'No publicity is bad publicity,' said Jack. 'If you want to get to the top Ashe, babe – there are some things you're going to have to get used to.'

I drank my drink in silence. I was starting to feel like a commodity.

'Oh, and look – can you wear that outrageous blue Klavin number again tonight?'

'I was going to get an early night, as a matter of fact. Like to recover from last night. Remember?'

'Just one little press party – to please me,' said Jack. 'Won't take more than half an hour, I promise. Just a couple of poses with you and Klavin to cement the "muse" story.'

'Is Ingrid going to be there?'

'No, Ingrid is not. Last thing I heard she was angling for an invitation to the Jean Paul Gaultier bash. After her scene with Klaus, rumour has it she's trying to switch allegiance.'

'OK, OK. What time do I have to be ready?'

I was whacked, actually, but it seemed that my

new status as Klavin's 'Super-Top' meant tiredness was one luxury I couldn't afford.

Twelve

Back at the hotel there was a package waiting for me. It was a big hard-sided photographer's envelope, so I guessed it was a load of Klavin shots to sort through for Marco.

I left it on the bed while I took a shower. After my shower I curled up under the duvet and opened it.

They weren't fashion shots. They were black and white photos of me, taken in the rain. Sasha's shots. I spread them out on the bed. I was absolutely knocked out by them . . .

I mean, they weren't glamorous or anything. They were just incredibly moving. He had caught something about me that I had never seen anyone do before. He had captured how I felt inside. It was me, stripped of all the make-up and the gloss. There were ones of me caught motionless as the crowd swept past me – like I was the one still moment in a mad-rushing world. And there was the one of me sitting in the sad little café – just a girl in an old mac looking as if life has never been so wonderful and so worth living, in spite of the rain running down her face . . .

There was a note, too. It was in Sasha's careful French handwriting. It said:

I thought you should have these. They are no use to me any more. They just remind me too much of you. Sasha.

I was on to Reception immediately.

'When was that package left for me?'

'About an hour ago. The young man didn't want to wait.'

I slumped dejectedly on the bed. '*No use to me any more*' – Why should he reject me like this? I tried to remember what I had done or said to him. But I had to admit I had hardly given him a thought in the last day or so, I'd been so busy, so wrapped up in myself. He must think I didn't care one bit. And then I remembered, with a sudden jolt. He must have seen the Press coverage, all that nonsense about me and Maurice. No-one could have missed that. And I had no way now of getting in touch to put him right. How had I allowed things to get in such a mess?

I felt a real jerk. There I'd been, partying all night, being spoiled rotten and meantime he was wearing out the soles of his shoes looking for a job and it was all my fault.

I started half-heartedly to get ready for the party. I did my make-up and then went to the closet to fetch the dress.

That was really odd. I could have sworn I left the dress hanging on its own on the right-hand side of the closet. Maybe I'd been mistaken. I searched through the rack of clothes. And then I double-checked. And double-checked once more. There was no doubt about it. It had gone. But nobody would have come into my room and just taken it. My eye fell on the French windows that led to the balcony. They were pushed closed but not locked. Had I left them open? I couldn't remember.

I walked on to the balcony. Ingrid's windows were open and there was just a tiny balustrade that divided our two balconies.

'What size is it?' – an echo of Ingrid's voice came back to me. It was size eight. That must be her size, too, of course.

I tried to suppress a growing conviction that Ingrid had 'borrowed' the dress.

'Ingrid, are you there?' I called.

There was no reply. It seemed she wasn't in her room. With determination, I climbed over the balustrade. There was one easy way to find out if the dress was in there.

'Ingrid,' I called again. She definitely wasn't in the bedroom and she wasn't in the bathroom either. I tiptoed over to her closet feeling like a burglar. A rapid search through the hangers didn't come up with the dress. I started to go through the drawers – the bottom drawer was really heavy. With a great heave I pulled it out.

I couldn't believe my eyes. It was absolutely stuffed with food. And, like, the most disgusting food. Great bags of sweets and patisserie, dozens of candy bars and a big tub of chocolate-nut spread. It was like the most fattening food you could imagine. And Ingrid was skinny as a bean, in spite of eating twice as much as me.

Then suddenly it all fell into place. Those trips to the loo. The red eyes. She must have been throwing up. Why hadn't I realised before. Ingrid must have a problem . . . it was obvious to me now – she was bulimic. She needed help.

I slowly got to my feet. Jeez – she really did have a problem – after all the scandal about Lisa, too. I started to push the drawer closed but it jammed.

That's when I heard the lift come to a stop at our floor. *Ingrid.*

At that moment my eye fell on the dress. So she *had* taken it, after all. It was reflected in her bathroom mirror – hanging on the back of her bathroom door.

I strode over and grabbed it by the hanger. I paused, but, frankly, I didn't feel up to confronting her right now. I shoved at the drawer again but it was really jammed.

Then I thought that maybe it would be a good thing if Ingrid realised someone knew about her problem. Perhaps then she would start to come to her senses. So I left the drawer as it was and made my escape back over the balcony.

I threw on the dress and finished my make-up, going over in my mind how it must feel to be Ingrid. She was having a pretty rough time by any standards – but she didn't have to take it out on me.

And then, just before I left, I took one more look at the photos scattered across my bed. They *were* brilliant. And it suddenly struck me: Julio was bound to be at the party. I gathered up the photos, slid them back into the envelope and took them with me.

The party was another of those posey formal do's. It was at the Ritz. I was getting to feel like I was overdosing on gilt and chandeliers. Anyway, I did all the right things, I guess. Jack was doing his usual round of introductions and I think I smiled in the right places and at the right people and into the right cameras. I put on a pretty impressive act of being 'Ashe the supermodel'. But all the time I was keeping one eye on the door for Julio to arrive.

He was one of the last to turn up. The minute he came through the door I made straight for him.

'Ashe, how is my Blue Angel?' he said.

'Can I ask you a favour?' I started.

'Can I refuse?'

'Could I ask you to look at some photographs and give an opinion?'

'You 'ave snaps? You are not coming over to my side of the camera, I hope. I don't want competition.'

'They're not mine. They're a friend's.

He frowned. 'Very well. Let me see.' As I fetched the envelope, it occurred to me that he must be pestered by people like this all the time.

Julio looked through the pictures with a serious expression on his face. Then he went back to the close-up of me in the café with the rain running down my face.

'I think you like this "friend" very much. Yes?'

'How can you tell?'

'You do not look like that at me.'

I could feel myself blushing.

'But what do you think of them, as pictures?'

'I think, if he has more shots like these, I would be interested to meet him.'

'Really? You're serious. Not just to please me?'

'Not in the least to please you. I am very jealous of this young man. Maybe I will want to have, how you say, a "duel" with him.'

He reached into his pocket and brought out a Press Pass. 'Give him this. I am very busy. But if he brings his work to the show tomorrow, I will find time to look at it.'

I gave him a big kiss on the cheek and he went off shaking his head.

'No more, you will have everyone talking about *us*.'

I pointed out to Jack that I'd done more than my promised half-hour and got away as soon as I could after that. As I hurried down the stairs to the lobby, I passed a load of people who had obviously come on from the Gaultier party. That's when I came face to face with Ingrid.

I gave her a meaningful look. She glanced at the dress and, obviously putting two and two together, flushed scarlet.

'You're leaving early,' she said.

'Maybe I'm afraid I'll turn into a pumpkin. Or my dress might dematerialise – again,' I said pointedly.

I took a cab back to the hotel, wondering how on earth I was going to get the Press Pass to Sasha. I had no idea where he lived – I didn't even have a phone number. And I didn't know anyone he knew either. Apart from at the restaurant. The charming patron was hardly likely to help me. And then I remembered the other, older, waiter. He had seemed friendly enough.

'Stop ici,' I said to the cab driver as I caught sight of the familiar Café-Brasserie sign.

It must have just closed up. All the chairs were stacked on the tables and the doors were locked too. I rattled them. A figure came out from the back and I saw I was in luck. The friendly waiter was coming over to me.

'Fermé,' he said, shaking his head and pointing at the sign hanging there.

I shook my head and rattled again. He unlocked the doors with a sigh.

'Eh bien?'

'Sasha.' I said waving the Press Pass.

'Il ne travaille plus ici.'

'Non. Do you know where he lives?'

He shook his head, not understanding.

'Son adresse?'

'Mais oui,' he said. Then he came out with an unintelligible load of French which sounded like: 'alors-il-habite-même-bâtiment-que-moi.'

'Can you give this – Donnez – à Sasha?'

'Bien sûr.'

'Ce soir?'

'Aucun problème.'

I indicated that I wanted a Biro and he brought one out from his pocket. I hesitated, then wrote on the back of the Pass.

Sasha – Your photographs are brilliant. I showed them to Iononi and he wants to see you at the show tomorrow with more of your work. I miss you so much. Till tomorrow. Will explain everything then – Ashe.

The waiter walked off, patting his pocket with the Press Pass in it, gesturing reassuringly that he would be sure to deliver it. I walked thoughtfully back to the hotel.

It was a hot night and there was not a breath of wind. I threw the windows wide open and sat on the floor leaning against the window-frame, staring out into the night. I kept going over and over in my mind the walk down the catwalk in those lethal platforms. It was some nightmare. What if I slipped at a crucial point and messed the whole finale up? From far below, the sound of the traffic droned and droned through my head. Didn't Paris ever sleep? Eventually, I guess I must have dropped off right there where I sat, because I awoke in a cold sweat. I was dreaming that I was sliding down some kind of endless glacier in the Klaus Klavin robe and all these flashlights were trained on me.

As I came to my senses I realised – that was really odd – flashlights *were* flashing in through my window. There was a bit of a commotion going on outside. I went out on the balcony and looked down. A small crowd had gathered and they were all staring up in my direction. There was a fire engine with its motor throbbing. Someone was shouting in French through a loudhailer and a spotlight was being directed up on to the roof above my room.

I turned and looked up and my heart missed a beat. Perched on an overhanging ledge that was built out over our rooms was *Ingrid*.

She was hanging on with one hand and shading her eyes from the glare with the other. I shouted at the policeman with the loudhailer. 'She doesn't understand French. Ne comprend pas,' I said. There was a moment's lull.

'You know 'er?' he shouted back.

'Yes.'

'Try and speak with her.'

I could see her tense figure caught in the shifting spotlight, but I couldn't reach her. I climbed up on a piece of parapet where I could get a better view. There was a sickeningly narrow ledge between us which was the only way across to where she was standing.

'Don't come near me or I'll jump,' she said in a broken voice.

'It's OK. I'm not coming any nearer.'

I cast a glance towards the ground. We were at a giddying height. The people down below looked tiny.

'Come back down, Ingrid. Please.'

'What for?' she said bitterly.

'It can't be as bad as all that.'

'You don't understand,' she sobbed.

'Maybe I do?'

'Yes, perhaps you do . . .' she practically spat the words at me. Then she started sounding off about the fact that Marielle wanted to see her in the morning.

'Somebody must have told her . . .' she finished acidly.

'Not me,' I said. 'On my word of honour, Ingrid, I haven't said a thing.'

'You haven't?'

'But it doesn't alter the fact that you need help.'

She didn't reply, she just sobbed.

'Look, trust me. I'll do anything.'

'Why should you?'

'I guess I don't know why. But I will.'

'Tell those people to stop shouting and shining that light in my eyes,' she said weakly.

'Sure. Right away.'

'But don't go away.'

I could see now that she was shaking from head to foot. Tiny little bits of the ledge she was standing on kept cracking off and falling with a sound like a mini landslide. At any point it looked as if the zinc underneath her could give away. I could hear the phone in my room ringing but I didn't dare leave her. I just had this feeling that as long as I could stay in contact I could keep her from jumping.

'I'm not going anywhere. I'm staying here with you.'

'Don't let anyone else near me or I'll do it,' she sobbed.

'No-one. I promise.'

I could see the Manager of the hotel in my room. I signalled to him to keep back.

The next thing I knew, a mobile was being thrust into my hand.

A voice from the telephone said in English: 'Keep calm. Just keep her talking. It doesn't matter what you say. Just keep contact. We are trying to get equipment that will reach her.'

So that's what I did. I didn't know what the hell to talk about but I just kept on talking. I guess somehow, I don't know why, I got into telling her about Cherie. Like Cherie had had this big successful modelling career but she'd kind of been left with nothing at the end. And that modelling was no big deal.

Ingrid interrupted and said some pretty forthright things at that point about how *I'd* had it all so easy.

Then I told her a thing or two about the struggles I'd had – all the catalogue stuff I'd done and being treated like dirt and about the creep who ripped me off for test shots.

At that point she cried a bit and then she kind of laughed. It was a dry, bitter sort of laugh.

'I've really messed up, haven't I? I couldn't even go through with this.'

'Know what would take real courage, Ingrid?' I said. 'Coming right back down – like now.'

She started shaking again.

'That's the thing. I can't. I can't move.'

The zinc gave a creaking sound as if it was about to tear.

There was just that ledge about six centimetres wide and three metres long between us.

I climbed higher on to the parapet. I'll never know to this day how I did it, but I held on tight with my left hand and edged towards her, holding out my right. I felt sick to my stomach doing it.

'Look,' I said. 'There's nothing to it. Just look straight ahead and walk towards me.'

She just stared at me dumbly.

'Don't look down, Ingrid. Just look at me. You can do it. I know you can.'

The zinc underneath her groaned again. I willed her to move. Then, as if sleepwalking, she walked steadily across the ledge towards me.

Closer and closer, step by step until . . . I had her hand in mine. I grasped it with all the strength I had.

Suddenly, there was a strong pair of arms around me. And it was all over. Somehow the firemen had lifted the two of us back down safely on to the balcony.

After that there seemed to be endless statements to be made – the place was swarming with police and firemen. Ingrid had slumped into a heap and a woman who looked like a doctor had given her an injection to calm her down and then taken her off, I don't know where. I was kind of in a daze. I just wanted peace and quiet to recover.

When they had all gone, I stood for a moment in the bathroom, wondering if I was going to throw up or not. I caught sight of my reflection in the mirror. The Klavin dress was torn and covered in lichen and stuff. It just hung there. Three bits of shiny blue fabric held together by big glittery fake crystal buttons – that's all it was.

Thirteen

Cherie used to have this saying when I was a kid: 'When something scares you – think of something worse.' You know, it works in a mad illogical kind of way – like it makes the scary thing you have to do not half so bad?

Well, when I arrived at the Carrousel next day, I took a long hard look at that catwalk. It was nothing. Compared to that ledge Ingrid had walked along last night, it was like a four-lane highway.

Backstage was something else. There are just two words that describe the scene in the changing room – the first is "chaos" and the second is "panic". We'd all had to turn up two hours early 'cos catwalk make-up takes like forever.

There was a sudden hush when I walked in. I guess some rumour of what had happened during the night must have got around. Several of the girls came over and asked if I was OK. And everyone wanted to hear about Ingrid.

I played the whole thing down. I just made out like Ingrid had a few problems to sort out and had made a bit of a scene – basically, the whole thing had been blown up out of all proportion.

We didn't have much time to chat, because hair and make-up wanted us clamped to our seats. Klavin had engaged this really classy make-up designer for the show and he had come up with an icy kind of look that made all the girls seem carved out of stone.

There was a team of make-up artists working under him – the girl I had was French and didn't speak a word of English. It was kind of a relief to be able to sit in silence and watch as she worked on my face. I'd never had a full-scale catwalk make-over before and it was totally different from photographic make-up. The stuff they used was heavier for a start. She worked for ages with different colours sculpting along the cheekbones in blue and mauve. And when she came to my eyes she used a big thick eyeliner brush and painted long lines sweeping from below the lower lashes and out beyond the sides of my eyes. She did the same with the upper lid. It looked pretty space-age from where I was sitting. But I guess with all the lights and stuff it would just look like great big eyes.

She had to work really fast. Basically it was like an all-out race to get us all done in time. As soon as she had done my face, another girl took over my hair. The hair girl really went to town, spraying my hair from the roots to the ends with translucent blue spray. I watched as she built it up and back as if it was being lifted by an invisible force – like wind was blowing through it. OK, so by the time she finished, I looked unreal – truly unreal! And the spray set so hard you could tap on it!

The tension was really building up as the seconds ticked away. The whole room seemed to be seething with legs and arms as girls climbed into tights and got zipped-in or laced-up or buttoned to by the dressers.

One girl was moaning that her shoes didn't fit. Her dresser was sent for inner soles. Another had laddered her tights. Everywhere there seemed to be last-minute panics. Another girl who was having her boots laced up wimpered in German for a paracetamol.

Then a couple of the Tops just wandered in – over one hour late. They strode in like royalty and everyone's attention was diverted to them. A whole army of make-up, hair and dressers descended on their little area.

Hortense was getting in a right old flap. She and the next-door dresser were having a good-natured kind of shouting match in rapid French. And then she was cut short. Silence had descended on the room. It was time! Michel was standing in the middle of the room with headphones on, waving his arms. Outside, the first members of the audience were beginning to arrive. From now on everyone was going to have to keep really quiet.

Tension crackled like electricity through the room. Katya tiptoed over and whispered: 'Good luck. Don't be nervous.'

And then all of a sudden the intro music started up.

'Here we go. Over the top!' whispered another girl taking a last drag off a cigarette held by her dresser. I joined the end of a tense line that led up to the wings.

When my turn came, I stepped on to the catwalk and, for just a split second, froze – like a rabbit caught in the headlamps of an oncoming car. And then Michel whispered 'Allez' and I was away.

My entrance was greeted by a tidal wave of applause which went to my head with a rush of adrenaline. I felt as if I was ten foot high. As I passed Katya, she grinned at me.

I got to the end of the catwalk, paused, turned, posed, and turned back again. I strode back and passed one of the Tops, who looked as if this was the most boring thing that she had ever done in her whole life.

The second time down the runway, I searched through the audience for Sasha. I was giving up hope when, just at the very end, I caught a fleeting glimpse of him. He was crushed in with the bank of journalists and he had his camera at the ready. He'd made it.

Back in the dressing room bedlam reigned. Between each elegant foray down the catwalk, we were all forced to change at a frenzied speed. All around there were muffled shrieks in a wild variety of languages of 'Shoes!', 'Merde!', 'I don't believe it!', 'Pronto!', 'Scarpe!!' 'Godverdomme.'

Each time back, Hortense just grabbed me and unzipped me with the skill of a nurse handling a baby. Before I knew quite what had hit me, I'd find I was in my next outfit and back in line. Somehow, against all the odds, the line never faltered and girl after girl headed out into the lights on time. By the fifth time I'd made it back without a hitch, I was actually starting to enjoy myself.

I had an extra few minutes to prepare for my finale entrance. Hortense shook out the folds of the dress and held it out for me.

As I slipped it on, it settled round me like a cloud. She slid the dreaded platforms on to my feet, secured the straps and then lifted the veil over my head. Carefully, I picked my way back to the entrance.

There was a pause in the music. You could have heard a pin drop as I waited in the wings. And then the finale number started up.

As the sinuous chords of the music flooded through the room a cloud of dry ice swept across the catwalk.

'OK, allez. Bonne chance,' whispered Michel.

There was an audible gasp from the audience as I swept down the runway. I felt, in actual fact, as though I was floating on air. It seemed, in those few seconds that it took to reach the end of the catwalk, that time was literally standing still.

I turned, lifted the veil, posed and caught the full force of the photographers' flashes. Then I swept back again. As I came level with where I had seen Sasha, I just paused again for an instant and turned to face him. A camera flashed. If instinct was anything to go by, he'd got the best shot of the show.

At the top of the catwalk I turned back to face the audience, the music came to a crescendo, a cloud of dry ice enveloped me and the special effects took over. Lasers lit up, seeming magically to replace me with a 3-D image of the Ange Bleu bottle. As I slid silently from the runway the music faded into silence, then the slogan came up: 'Ange Bleu – woman or illusion?'

There was deafening applause after that. Klaus came rushing in, sweat running down his face, beaming from ear to ear. He grabbed me by the hand and one of the Tops by the other and, almost before I knew it, we were striding down the catwalk with a long line of the other girls pouring after us.

The audience loved it. They were rising from their seats giving Klaus a standing ovation. I breathed a sigh of relief. Unbelievably, against all the odds, nothing had gone wrong.

Back in the changing room the Press started to flood in. I just managed to get a T-shirt over my head before I had a guy shooting pictures right in my face.

Hortense was waving her fist at them but none of the photographers took a blind bit of notice of her. They were all fighting to get at me.

'Ashe . . . Ashley . . . Ashe . . . Over here . . . Smile . . .' came at me like a kind of chorus. And then, way back, crushed behind two guys with lights and video cameras, I caught sight of Sasha.

In two seconds I had dodged through the crowd and was at his side.

'Hi! I've got to talk to you.'

'Not here,' he said. 'Can't we go somewhere quieter.'

'Where? I've only got half an hour, at the most.' A photographer was trying to get a shot of us together.

'There's a café, La Corona, behind the Louvre, by the Seine.'

I shook my head. 'We'll get mobbed. Somewhere quieter.'

'The church . . .' said Sasha. 'They'll never think of looking there.'

We were getting thrust apart by a flood of well-wishers coming in from the audience. A load of people were already heading off to the Press party.

'L'Eglise Saint Germain L'Auxerrois . . .' I managed to catch. 'It's just across from the café . . .'

P.S.

The stillness of the church was almost unearthly after the hubbub of the show. As I walked down the long aisle, I could hear my footsteps echoing on the ancient flagstones. An old woman was at work polishing the brasswork on the altar. The whole place smelled of time and age.

'I'm here,' said a voice and Sasha emerged from the shadows.

'Did you see Iononi?'

'I did. And, well . . . You are looking at his new third camera assistant – on trial, of course.'

'But that's wonderful!'

'It's a very important position. I will be allowed to change his film.'

'But it's a start. Isn't it?'

'Yes. And that is why I am here to thank you. It is, as you say, awesome.' He paused.

'Could we sit down?' I pleaded. 'My feet are killing me.'

'Are you sure you have the time?'

'What do you mean "the time"?'

'Don't you have to rush back to all your glamorous friends?'

'Not right now. Right now, I want to be with you.'

'What about your new boyfriend?'

'What new boyfriend?'

He brought a page of newspaper out from his pocket and pointed to the picture of me and Maurice.

'Oh, you mean Maurice. You didn't look at the picture very carefully, did you?'

He shrugged. 'How do you mean?'

'If you'd looked more carefully you would have seen that he didn't have his arm round me. He had his arm round the *back* of me. He has his arm around the guy on the other side – look you can just see his hand – there.'

Sasha leaned forward and studied the picture.

'Are you sure?'

'The two of them live together.'

'So it's not a big romance, like everyone says?'

'I think three would be a bit of a crowd, don't you?'

He screwed the paper into a ball and smiled to himself. Then he gave me a sideways look.

'So you still haven't found a boyfriend?'

I shook my head. He drew closer and put an arm around me.

'Would you consider a third camera assistant?'

'I think a third camera assistant would be just about perfect. I reckon we've both got a big future ahead of us.'

'Do you think it is all right to kiss here? It is God's house. He sees everything. We should behave, non?'

'What do you think?'

'I think if people truly love each other, God would maybe close His eyes, just for one moment . . .'

What happened to Marco's other models? Did Chrissie hit the headlines? Did Zoë ever catch up with Mark? Find out in Havana to Hollywood – Zoë's story . . .

HAVANA TO HOLLYWOOD

Chloë Rayban

All I'd ever wanted to do was act – and at last I'd landed the part of my dreams . . .

But when the Cariba shoot took me to Cuba, I had to give up the part that meant so much to me – and possibly the person, too . . .